Avalon Blue's Quest

By Patsy Stanley

ISBN 978-1- 7332437-0-4

Library of Congress Control Number: 2019908636

More books by Patsy Stanley:

Novels:
Addition Jones
An Older Wine-Short stories
Emerald Hawks Flight
Avalon Blue's Quest

Illustrated books for all age readers:
Christmas Stories From the Crone's Castle
The Dreadful Noises of Landoshar

Native American:
Red Leaf
The Green Mountain Shaman

Energy books-Metaphysical:
The Mental Body
The Spiritual Nature of Atomic Structure
Sound Energies
Shield Energies
Chakras, Meridians, and the Color Energies
The Elements

The World's Work Does Not Wait to be Done by Perfect People...

"We are so accustomed to disguising ourselves to others, that in the end, we become disguised to ourselves." F. de la Rochefoucauld

"The usual hero adventure begins with someone from whom something has been taken, or who feels there is something lacking in the normal experience available or permitted to the members of society. The person then takes off on a series of adventures beyond the ordinary, either to recover what has been lost or to discover some life-giving elixir. It's usually a cycle, a coming and a returning."

- Joseph Campbell, "The Hero with a Thousand Faces"

Throughout history, many indigenous cultures have managed their spiritual lives with animal teachers, or totem as mentors. Their storytellers, long before languages were written, used tattoos, rituals, and a variety of other means to teach the lessons to be learned. The idea may seem archaic today, yet the shaman women on the secret island taught us more flexible ways to learn; our souls were their students. We know of at least eight learning styles at present. No doubt more are waiting for discovery as humanity pushes forward...

Table of Contents

The Travelers

The scent of wood smoke drifted lazily through the cool night air, mixing pleasantly with the sweet smell of hay and the soft, contented nickering of horses. She sat motionless in the turquoise and red Traveler's wagon, waiting, listening to the soft murmur of the few people still gathered around the central fire. She listened until the final voice drifted away.

Now and then an errant breeze moved an edge of the dark red curtains over the small window above the table usually latched into its place in the wall. The table was down, a pot of tea resting on its shiny red surface. A half dozen teacups rested in a small wood box nearby.

Traveler clans were judged by their ritual tea sets, particularly their cups of clay, porcelain or metal, which often bore faces, gemstones cannily placed, or silver bottoms. The half dozen ritual cups in the wood box had been in her family for generations. One of the cups was covered with hand painted flowers in bold, bright colors. The flowers looked as though they were going to bloom into a living bouquet any second. She picked the cup up and turned it round in her hands. Red poppies from the meadow and purple alliums bloomed bright and strong on its surface. There wasn't a place for things less brave or valiant.

Garib Cantibo, her father, tall, broad shouldered, dark haired with flashing brown eyes, handsome in his black silk shirt, had humbly sipped his ritual tea from this cup the night of his betrothal to Alician Bo Bellesian. Her mother was the only person, other than the Traveler Elders, to whom he might ever humble himself. She and the Lost Ones.

They were called Gary and Alice Smith, and she was Elagin Seaway Cantibo, called Elaine Smith, their only child, to the world outside their band of Travelers. Her mother chose the matriarchal dark blue water cup with silver lines woven over the surface for her part of the betrothal ritual.

The water cup represented the lineage of Estellina Bo Coursay, her grandmother, whose people traveled here from an island long ago and far away, an island steeped in legend, secrets, magic, and rituals. An island where shaman women trained their character to its best since time out of mind. It was whispered that shaman women had trained on the secret island since the Old Moon left and the New Moon took its place and gave its approval.

Alice and Elagin were descended from a Shamanic lineage that believed much of spiritual growth was gifted to humans through animal Elders. Their island ancestors tattooed animal totem and symbols on each other, developing rituals around their beliefs that animals were spirit messengers, guides, and protectors. They believed animals brought lessons to teach humans. They believed animal tattoos held power to embolden and draw forth transformations of the soul.

Both humans and animals agreed on this; and over time, the power of their combined beliefs caused the tattooed lines on their shamanic students to gain spirit life and begin to move.

In time, the moving, scrolling lines of animal tattoos given in secret ceremonies created a bridge between the animal teacher and the person, transmuting the higher spiritual values of the animal to the human. Each animal tattoo identified a spiritual belief or lesson a human soul was in the process of learning. The living tattoo guided their soul's character development.

Some of the women on the mysterious island stayed and took new names and worked with the shamans and animal Elders. Many of their new names incorporated seasons, weather, or animals.

After the lesson was learned, just as in childbirth, the lines faded away and disappeared through a powerful spiritual chemical discharge, a magic overseen by the animal Elders. The lines came back only as brief reminders, when a path was forgotten, for their investment in the spiritual nature of each human was life long.

*

The silver lines moved up across Elagin's face as they did whenever she became emotional instead of her matter-of-fact, calm, shamanic self. She planned from long ago to use the same water cup her mother had used for her engagement ritual.

Elaghin's eyes roamed the small wagon that was her home. Her father had spoke often of their heritage, saying with a laugh that their homes were earth-bound ships on wheels; he said Nomads, Gypsies, Travelers, Migrants, Wanderers and the like have always lived happily in these kinds of homes.

Her mother's black eyes had flashed with laughter and appreciation when her father spoke of such things. Elagin never grew tired of watching the silver legends, the beautiful, scrolling lines of living art moving and resettling themselves again and again into new scenes over her mother's arms, neck, and face.

Elagin went to the small, red framed mirror hanging from a nail above the table and looked at herself. She smoothed thick black hair back with one hand, retied it at the nape of her neck with a red silk band. Large, gold hoops swung from her shell shaped earlobes. She moistened her full red mouth and studied the swarthy smoothness of her high cheekbones and the fine shine in her black eyes. She was big and dark and tall. She wore dignity and gracefulness like a mantle swinging through a star lit night sky. It was true. She liked herself.

A discreet knock on the door interrupted her thoughts. He was there, separated from her only by the oak door. Her hand flew to her heart. She took a deep breath, strode to the door in the back of the wagon and opened it wide so he could step in. His large, bold presence filled her small home. His black eyes sparkled like diamonds as he smiled down at her.

"Lucas Blizzard Solestone," she stated his proper name solemnly, with a smile that nearly blinded him. He gave a pleased laugh of relief as she took his hands in hers and led him to the table. He could almost tell how this query was going to go. His suspense would soon be over. He hoped he would win her, so the other two men vying for her hand would have to look elsewhere.

He sat down on one side of the red lacquered table. She sat down on the other side. He looked around at the strong, proud memories of her parents everywhere; it was as if they were watching them. Reminders of other relatives were placed around the room, as well. An ancestral shawl draped around the cross hanging on the wall; a pair of shoes on the floor pointed forward towards the open road at the front of the wagon. All he surveyed was an unspoken statement that this ritual was being overseen by her absent parents.

Luke chose the same cup her father once chose. She poured the tea, the flowers bloomed and the water ran, and they drank together. Then she wiped the cups and placed them back in the old, varnished box. The cup didn't crack or break and he never choked on his tea.

Elagin's ancestors approved of Lucas Blizzard Solestone. Now he could ask her to marry him. They both stood. He laughed in open appreciation of the silver lines scrolling and rolling upon her flushed face.

"You're a magic woman!" he exclaimed. He swept her into his arms. She was big boned and tall, almost as tall as he was. They looked into each other's eyes as he chanted the ancient words of proper engagement to her, finishing with "....and wherever thee travels, will thou forever think of us and keep our breadth and twain in thy own making?" He finished and stopped speaking, waiting for her answer.

She finished the ritual words for him, joyously, gladly. "...and thee shall give just cause forever to us and ours."

She smiled at him and, as was proper, he nodded and left, his face jubilant. She closed the door behind him and went to the long, narrow cupboard holding her clothes. She took out her wedding dress, unfolded it and held it up. Handmade in the traditional Traveler's wedding pattern, she remembered the thousands of tiny stitches she'd taken in the making of the simple silk and cotton black wedding dress over the years. His name was worked into every stitch, had been, from the first stitch taken when she was seven and still awkward with a needle. She'd pricked her finger and a drop of blood had melted into that first stitch. She remembered blushing, the silver lines scrolling up her young face. She knew the drop of blood was an omen.

Their blood was bound together. She never named him to anyone, not since she started her wedding dress. To name him would have brought bad luck. But everybody knew anyway.

She ran her fingertips over the cleanly edged sleeves and the modestly cut neckline. The jet-black material rustled satisfactorily. She slipped the dress over her head and it settled into place. She placed her hands on her wide hips and whirled around until the full skirt flew out in a lovely arc.

Silver lines rose up in thin, delicate patterns across her dark throat, face and arms. When she stopped dancing, the skirt hem, with a last sigh and whisper, settled into place just above her ankles. She laughed, slipped out of her wedding dress and slid it onto a hanger. Then she opened the back door and hung it from the wood brace running under the outside eaves at the back of the wagon to announce her betrothal.

Everyone would see it in the morning and knock loudly on the sides of her wagon to give her good luck. Later, she would find small containers of salt on the ground outside the wagon to throw to keep bad luck away.

Then the women would visit, each one bringing her a square of cloth about the size of a handkerchief to sew on her wedding dress. The beautiful pieces of linen, cotton, silk and other materials came from their ancestors and relatives past weddings, funerals, and other rituals.

Elagin and the women sewed the center point of each piece of material onto the wedding dress while retelling its history. The slips of material swung freely from their centers, floating in textures, patterns, and colors, filling the wedding dress with stories.

Sometimes there were so many they hid the black wedding dress beneath.

Wearing the women's history of her Travelers clan, each piece of cloth accompanied the bride as she walked to her wedding. Thus, many ancient women of long ago, back in a time of travel and magic beyond reckoning, awed the Travelers at the wedding with their whispered stories. Soft and aged, the pieces of cloth murmured and hummed the ancestral songs from their Traveler's families. They whispered protections and advices, a part of something ancient and powerful invited with respect and honor to another Traveler's wedding.

After the wedding, the bride packed the cloth squares and her black wedding dress carefully into the sturdy, fleece lined crate in the bottom of her closet.

The dress would be passed on to her children and their generations to keep the old stories of their Traveler's heritage alive.

Broadcloth is dense, usually wool, requiring the utmost of labor to draw the yarns into a less dense drape. A grim fabric, but at least you need not hem it.

Chapter 1.   My Friend Harry

Okay. It's my fault I have to stay away from people. I admit it. I borrowed trouble, and it forced me to become a traveling hermit. Since I left the island, only Aunt Amelia ever saw my condition, and now she is dead. Not from shock, though, from old age.

I have a stack of journals in the closet, all written since my enforced isolation began. Yes, there is more than one journal. That's how long it's been. I started out writing "Dear Diary" in each journal like a simpering young girl, but since I have somehow survived into old age, I decided to write to the elusive Harry Houdini instead. He worked with magic and kept secrets, just as I must do now.

People say I am naïve, always have been, always will be. Maybe so, but I am damn good at keeping secrets, just like Harry Houdini was. People think you have to be smart to keep a secret, but that's not true. I keep a secret every day of my life. Since I can't do anything about it, I disappear whenever I need to, sort of like Harry Houdini did. It's simple. I follow his example. I pack up and move on.

*

Winter's Lee. The weather is constantly changing in this gloomy place. It's raining tonight. It's been raining off and on all day. I never know when the rain will stop or start. There are no solid indicators for me to see, like there seems to be for the people living here. I wait to see them sniff the air or stare up at the sky, but they don't. Somehow they disappear just before the skies open up, leaving me standing out in the rain, wondering where and how the hell they all disappeared. I carry an umbrella now. Live and learn.

I don't think I will ever understand the doings of this grim geography, this dark, northern seacoast village with its violent, stormy, foggy weather. The people living here are taciturn, damp people who practice the greatest economy of speech, often using one syllable to express a whole sentence, an opinion, or to make their usual general comment. No newspaper needed.

Anyway, after I was forced to live in extreme loneliness, but not poverty, for a long time, I became desperate, so I turned to writing so I could spill my guts and not get found out. You see, Aunt Amelia was the only one who knew my secret, and she's gone now but she didn't take my secret with her.

To compensate for my lack of writing skills, for I am not a natural author, I developed an ornate handwriting style using purple ink.

I search for journals in out-of-the-way places, bookshops or antique stores. My current journal came from the bookshop in the village. It has a dark blue cover with sheets of fine, thin vellum inside. When I'm feeling good the purple ink dances across the vellum as though the pen and paper were made for each other. In darker moods, there are slashes and crashes of clinging words trying to survive.

I ended up in Winter's Lee simply because it was time to move on again. I was being noticed. At the time, I closed my eyes, stuck my finger on a map and it settled on "Winter's Lee." The name sounded cool, insular, far away from people, exactly what I needed to accommodate my secret. I planned to stay in Winter's Lee just a short time, then move on as usual. That was in the beginning.

I rented a room at the See Shells Motel on the beach below the tall, black cliffs. I guessed it was not a misspelling, for there were shells everywhere. It stormed like hell hath no fury the first night. I had my usual luck, so of course, my tiny room faced the sea. I huddled on the lumpy bed in my basil and purple-striped security pajamas and pink bunny house shoes, listening to the thunder of the sea and the rain beating against the walls and window of my room. Or should I say cage. That's what it felt like.

I smoothed my hands over every place I could reach on my body to calm them down. No animal or human likes being isolated in a dinky little room on the edge of the sea in dangerous weather! The roar of the storm was deafening, but I couldn't risk leaving. I looked around and mused. *Maybe this room will end up being my coffin. My own personal version of Davy Jones' locker complete with dingy dark brown drapes and a too-soft mattress.* I was terrified, but what if I left and someone saw them? I couldn't risk it.

I hunkered down, angry and scared, to wait out the long, miserable night. I soothed all the places I could reach on my body. Thoughts of how it was okay to die off because I was old ran through my mind, just in case it happened.

At last I fell into uneasy dreams in which I searched frantically for a lime green, elusive life raft. I woke up at the crack of dawn with a sleep deprived hangover. The fierce storm was over. *I hope it got what it came after,* I thought angrily.

I needed to clear my head. I decided to go for a walk on the beach. I pulled on one of my body leotards. They cover me from neck to wrists to ankles. That's why I wear them. I pulled a tunic over the leotard, finished dressing and stepped outside.

The morning air was heavy with the fishy scent of water. The beach was gray and waterlogged. I picked my way around the shells and other storm tossed flotsam on the sand. The light was white and thin, the kind of moody light I imagined artists yearn for when they want to paint something dramatic. The roar of the sea filled my ears. The wind blew damply, still heavy with water.

I pulled up the hood of my coat and marveled at how stern and cold the black waves were in this northern place. I imagined the nature beings governing this part of the world were larger and more austere than elsewhere. They wouldn't have the softness and humor of the smaller, quicker-natured beings living in the more tropical climates.

The beach grew rougher as I strolled along. I climbed over steep rocks and up onto a huge black boulder. I stood on top of it watching the black sea crashing against the shore. I looked around from my vantage point. The small strip of beach disappeared a few yards past the boulder I stood on.

My eyes scanned the tops of the tall black cliffs the beach disappeared into. I mouthed a silent *Wow!* A giant house sat close to the cliff's edge. I wondered who lived up there. No doubt it was someone with a flair for dark drama or a love of precipitous, stark realities. I imagined a dark history ran in their ancient, gothic family, no doubt including murders, and minor mayhem.

I wanted to see more of that incredible house, but I couldn't find a way to go any farther. I gave up, climbed down from the boulder and brushed myself off. My boots were wet. It was time to go back.

Rayon is a lightweight fabric tending to drape well over anything, especially lamp shades.

Chapter 2. Windbay Cottage

The days flew by. I found myself tarrying at the See Shells Motel. As soon as I returned from the beach, I exchanged my tiny room facing the sea for a larger one on the backside of the motel. My second night was much more comfortable.

The people in the quaint little village didn't pay much attention to me. Nobody asked any questions. Maybe they were used to weirdly dressed tourists, or just too insular to give a damn. Either way, it was a relief to stay in one place longer than usual, so I filled my days with exploring.

*

I discovered Windbay Cottage when a storm forced me to take a short cut back to the motel on the beach. I dawdled too long at the old bookshop in the village, and when I stepped out the door, the sky was dark and filled with rumbling clouds. A fierce storm was brewing. I wasn't surprised. Sudden storms and rain were part of the permanent temperament of this gloomy, gothic looking place. I stood outside the bookshop's long, recessed windows studying the dark, menacing clouds overhead. The storm was going to break soon.

Then I remembered the motel owner telling me about a shortcut. She said it was a path that ran "as the crow flies." I didn't have a clue as to how a crow flies.

"Okay....as the crow flies," I muttered to myself. The first drops of rain spattered to the sidewalk, delivering into the air the delicious sound and smell of new rain. The rich smell of freshly wetted dust mixed with the particles of scuffed shoe soles rose from the street. I stood, sniffing with abandon, forgetting where I was until someone brushed past me and said, "Huh!" probably in surprise at my standing in the rain staring up at the sky like a foolish goose with its mouth open.

I shut my mouth and hurried down the street trying to remember the shortcut to the motel. The rain came down harder. I rushed through it, not knowing where I was. In a few minutes the rain became sparse and fitful. I stopped to catch my breath and get my bearings. Amazed, I turned in a slow circle. I was standing in a neighborhood old beyond time. I was surrounded by magic, mysterious scents and earthy wisdom.

Earthy magic infused the air with the scent and feel of timeless covenants. I found myself strolling along under ancient trees forming shady green arches above broken sidewalks. Daisies, roses, lavender and herbs grew wild in yards of weathered houses looking like they were there since the dawn of time. Scents filled the air with floral perfumes. Bird houses and wren's nests were tucked among branches and odd places. Hummingbirds worked hollyhocks while busy brown wrens flickered shyly and hid behind tree leaves.

I wandered through deep, rain-washed silence, inspecting everything with my eyes. Nothing missed my attention, from the leaf laying on the uneven sidewalk, to the tender, huge white blossoms decorating a tall, stately, thick leafed tree.

Time was endless in this magic place. Time held no meaning, for clocks didn't exist. Sages, ancients, and all manner of elemental folk ruled this kingdom. Everyone living here was full of the wisdom accrued and passed down through their kinships. *All was well in the Kingdom, Amen.*

I picked my way across the crooked, crumbling, mossy old sidewalks. Then I stopped. My eyes were burning and something else was wrong. I blinked and looked down.

The right strap of my new purple flats had torn loose. I examined the torn strap. There was no way to fix it right now. I would just have to walk slower. I felt sweat searing my eyes, and hastily fished a tissue out of my pumpkin shaped orange purse, wiped my eyes and danced a bit until they quit stinging. I tried to pat my hair down. It frizzes in humidity. I fished in my pocket and found my red sweatband from the Coastal Fridge Boutique in the village and slipped it over my hair. You can't go wrong with red on red hair. So what if I'm sort of sixtyish and it came out of a bottle? Odd sorts of old people have rights, too, don't they? Someone somewhere should be glad I decided against purple hair. I don't know who, but someone.

Eyes dry, hair and thoughts tamed again, I looked around. Fairytale cottages, mysterious Victorians and staid, solemn wood or brick homes surrounded me. Rambling, cobbled walks curved through yards leading up to solemn porches filled with antique furniture; behind them, leaded glass windows glinted in ornate doors.

Ferns, vines, vegetables and flowers filled the yards. Trees and shrubs were allowed to grow into their natural height and shape. Small brown rabbits, birds, and bird baths dotted the yards. Wind chimes tinkled, drawing fairies to them. Bird houses drew in gnomes and moths. Great knots in the bases of the oldest trees encased the trolls' homes underneath them. I imagined a tiny undine sitting on a leaf playing a flute while drifting to the ground on a breeze.

I strolled on, mesmerized, until the magic of the neighborhood abruptly ended at the corner of a thin gray street leading back into the village. A two story cottage occupied the corner of the street, marking the end of the old magic and the beginning of the new world. The cottage bore an old wood sign in the tiny front yard.

"Windbay Cottage-For Sale."

Tall grass almost covered the faded sign. I peered past it at the cottage.

"Windbay Cottage."

I tested the name on my tongue. My eyes measured the skinny gray sidewalk wandering towards the front porch. The house was silvered with age. The porch was bare. The place looked old, peaceful, empty, and sad. Well, I could identify with that. Not the peaceful part, but the rest.

I studied the cottage, rocking back and forth on my heels under a huge oak tree shading the tiny front yard. Tall grass and wildflowers bloomed wherever they pleased. Dandelions, rampant with yellow courage, dotted the small front lawn, not giving an elf's belch if the house was occupied or not. Overgrown bushes hid recessed rectangles of windows, secreting them. The scent of roses floated from the back of the cottage, filling the front yard, wafting past me. I sniffed. Heavenly!

I looked around. I didn't see any "No Trespassing" signs or people. I may have trespassed a few times before, so I sort of knew the ropes. I hummed a nonchalant tune and wandered up the sidewalk, then strolled up the steps of the front porch like a door to door saleslady. But the scent of roses led me right back down the steps to the back of the cottage. Hundreds of red and white roses drooped over the broken fence and gate to the back yard.

I shoved on the broken gate until it gave way enough to let me squeeze through into the back yard and looked around. My hands twitched. I hummed louder. I felt an almost uncontrollable urge to water the roses. I NEEDED to dig in this dirt and find the hidden roots and bulbs, to unearth the magic stored back here.

I waded through high weeds, my eyes searching out every nook and cranny needing my help. I spied an old potting shed near the back door. It held flower pots, rakes and shovels. I scanned the yard again until I found the outline of the long ago garden. The garden was once a good size. It would be easy to dig up. I could see it filled with green beans, red tomatoes, and blue morning glories.

Suddenly I dropped the rake I was holding like a hot potato. The happy trance I was in, broke. Why, I couldn't put down roots here! I was doomed to live a nomad's life because of my secret! I must never forget that. Yes, I would have to move on soon. I moaned.

But I NEEDED to water the overflow of roses in this back yard! I NEEDED to sip my morning coffee standing at the back door gazing at the fertile, vegetable-filled garden while admiring the tall graceful ferns draping the tiny, falling down arbor I renovated. At least hoped to.

I shoved my way through the broken gate and hurried out front to study Windbay Cottage again. The front of the cottage looked out on a narrow street the tourists used in the summer to get to the village, but both sides and back lay in the magic neighborhood.

I frowned in concentration. Tourists never visited this part of the world except for the three short months that constituted Winter's Lee summer. For nine months or more, the cottage would have few, if any, curious eyes passing by. I gazed up at the tall, stately oaks standing like protective giants over the cottage. They looked like they had been standing on this spot forever. I felt included in their magnanimous protection. I wanted this home, this respite, no matter the cost.

"Windbay Cottage,'" I murmured the name to myself again and again, a habit I have that keeps my memory alert and me remembering where I am. You have to do stuff like that when you're aging. Anyway, it works.

*

Windbay Cottage was part of an estate. Mrs. Dublin, the estate manager, showed me through it. The front door opened into a charming foyer leading straight into a spacious living room.

"Land's sake! I don't know why you want it! It was Old Sam's place, and he was lost, him and his boat, in that big storm a few years ago! They say the place is haunted! That's why nobody wants it! He was my uncle ya' knaw!"

Mrs. Dublin spoke in exclamations while I roamed the inside, avidly taking in every detail. Windbay Cottage was larger than it looked from the street. The layout was clever, the workmanship exquisite. The floors, walls, and ceilings were covered in pale woods in pleasant patterns. A large bathroom with a big window lay to the east side of the cottage overlooking the backyard. There were bedrooms on each side of the bathroom. The kitchen's lofty plank ceiling peaked in the middle. A back door opened out onto a screened-in porch. Three sturdy wood steps with rusty side rails led down into the back yard. The dining room was filled with windows, sunlight pouring through them.

The second floor turned out to be an unfinished attic, a cavernous space with a vaulted ceiling and two huge windows—one in front, one in back. The unfinished walls were filled with rows of raw wood supports. A grimy floor hid beautiful, shiny wood. I ran to the dusty front window, scrubbed a hole in the grime and looked out.

"Beautiful!" I exclaimed, looking down on the tiny front lawn, then up into the vast, leafy boughs of the oaks towering green and sane over the yard and cottage, casting their mysterious shadows and sensible, cooling shade.

"I don't see what's sa' purty about it!" Mrs. Dublin retorted from behind me. "And would ya' mind tellin' me why yer' wearin' that turban thing around yer' head? And where did ya' ever find that odd colored tunic shirt thing? I'm wonderin' if ya' aren't some kind of Eccentric, ya' knaw?"

For a minute I froze. My heart sank. I turned around. Mrs. Dublin was wearing a tiny grin on her face. And, she didn't say a word about the leotard I was wearing under "that tunic shirt thing."

Cotton Voile is a lovely, light fabric suitable for the light of heart to swing and sway in.

Čhapter 3. The Heart's New Camp

The day came when at last the deed and the key to Windbay Cottage in my hands. I held them as if they were butterflies that might flit away any second. I ignored the congratulations and turned toward the cottage. I couldn't get there fast enough. I waded through green grass sluiced with thick molasses on my way across the yard. After what seemed like an eternity, I sort of bounded up the front steps, across the porch, and shoved the key into the worn lock. The door swung wide like it was waiting just for me. Its squeak sounded like, "You're home!" The key chain lay cool across my wrist for a second.

"I may love you," I murmured to the cottage. "Time will tell."

I stepped inside and wandered through the rooms that were now mine.

*

Mrs. Dublin sent over the local paint crew, carpenters, and a plumber. They set to work on all aspects of Windbay Cottage as though they were building a new ship. They didn't ask me anything. They knew what needed to be done. That was fine with me. They scraped and measured and shouted to each other while they worked on "Old Sam's" place.

They worked inside until the wood floors were pale again, shiny with varnish. The kitchen and dining room walls were fresh in coats of pale yellow paint. White baseboards gleamed under luminous wood ceilings. The ancient, white enamel range stayed in its place of honor. The claw foot tub also stayed in its place in the middle of the bathroom floor with a discreet shower stall added behind a wall.

The front and back doors now have stained glass windows matching the rest of the fairytale dwellings in this neighborhood. I reasoned *that I needed to keep it inviting for the little elemental families living here-don't want them packing their bags and moving away!*

The bedrooms are shore sand beige with white trim. The windows have sheer white curtains with sand-colored, pull-down shades behind them. There are thick, tan rugs on the plank floors. The rugs are the pretend sand beaches for the sea colored coverlets on the double beds.

The living room sofa and large easy chairs carry the same sand beige and white color themes with accents of sea-colored pillows. A water fountain and large sea shells placed here and there complete the picture; after all, what is living without water symbols for someone like me?

The attic smells like old secrets. The newly insulated walls are pale green. Colorful rugs dot the large, shiny yellow pine floor. Floor lamps and a red leather chair near the fireplace make it cozy. I left the two huge windows bare to gain all the natural light I could. One window overlooks the backyard, the other, the tiny front yard and street leading into the village. I set up work spaces under each window to make the most of the natural light.

I placed the large table I use to design body leotards and tunics under the back window. Nearby are shelves filled with fabrics, some bordering on fantastic. It took me a long time to find materials I like, and I'm very particular about them. After I design each leotard and matching tunic, I mail them to Mrs. Grimwood and her team to put together. She adds decorations or changes the fit. She has made so many leotards and tunics for me that she is used to my body and my fanciful need for extra "exclaiming" touches.

Sometimes I light the fire and draw the red leather chair close to it and dream dreams of what could be. Though older now, I still chew gum, drink a little red wine, and sometimes cuss; I remain a hopeful woman.

*

The work on Windbay Cottage moved outside. The silvered wood got scraped within an inch of its life, primed, then painted a soft yellow with blue trim. Blue wood shutters the color of the sea on a sunny morning frame the deep-set windows. The front and back yards stay trimmed, raked, and pruned. The backyard now has a high, curved gate and a white, sturdy wood fence for the roses to climb over. Green beans and wild daisies grow in the freshly turned garden. The arbor has a new bench, water fountain, and wind chimes. The postage stamp size front yard stays neatly mowed and bordered by a sturdy white picket fence with a gate in it.

The workers filled Windbay Cottage with good wishes for me. They sorted out my ways while they worked and began coaching me in how they expected me to act if I was to become an authentic "Eccentric" to them, making my ways acceptable. I need their acceptance and good will. It gives a meeting ground where our natural differences are buffered. I can hide in safety here. Being older and eccentric is not new to these crusty folks.

I know I am taking a huge risk by putting down roots in Winter's Lee. In the past, I worked endlessly to be a good person for my family. But this is now, and I can't go back. I have to go forward. Humanity hasn't evolved much in some ways. For those of us who don't fit in, it is wise to stay hidden and wary, because often times we are hated. So there's my biggest fear, Harry Houdini. That's where it lies...

*

I've never run across anyone I knew from the life I lived before I went to the island, not knowing what it was I was committing to, and returned changed forever in ways I have to keep hidden from my old world.

I maintain contact with my children and the few friends remaining from my old days. I think about them, but never visit and never give them a chance to visit me. I send them a postcard when I'm leaving town. I know they wonder about me and are hurt by my distancing, but that's the way it has to be since I left the island bound by spiritual rituals holding me hostage.

*

A package arrived from Mrs. Grimwood. In it was a new swamp-green tunic with matching leotard. Inch long embroidered silver marsh reeds curve around the ankles and wrists. Matching tiny silver reeds grace the neckline. Recently, I purchased a thin silver belt to go with it in anticipation. Great Aunt Amelia

30

would have loved it. She's who started me learning about fabrics and designing leotards and tunics.

Yes, the leotards and tunics all came about because of Great Aunt Amelia, who tricked me into going out on quest to find and tame my soul's insistent misery so I could get to the joy beyond it. I would have run screaming through an arid, thousand mile desert, across highways and byways, through tunnels and past diners with irresistible apple pie had I known what lay in store me, but such is the mystery of all spiritual journeys that karma compels the soul to be curious. Forget about apple pie, and go investigate. Nosy thing!

Windbay Cottage, my attic room with a fire in the fireplace on cold, rainy nights, fine vellum to write on, a hot cup of tea, all pleasant compensations provided by Aunt Amelia.

Sometimes I curl up in the high-backed red leather chair by the fireplace and return in time and conjure up Aunt Amelia's tall thinness, wide mouth and amazing, laughing generosity. Sometimes I stay small in the big red chair, watching the dancing flames. Silence is a familiar, constant companion.

*

"What shall I do with this absurdity O heart, O troubled heart, this caricature of age tied to me?"

The small, curvy woman past sixty murmured Yeats' famous lines as she stared out the front attic window of Windbay Cottage, one minute looking like a lost waif, the next looking older than anyone's grandmother would ever be. Like a trapped, intelligent animal, she stared out into the blustering, arguing rain, waiting for the silver lines to recede.

From habit she ignored the few raindrops blowing through the open window when the breeze changed, dampening the window sill and the floor. The dampness caused her fine orange halo of hair to stand up in a short, frizzy promenade framing her heart-shaped face. She stared out at the rain with prominent gray eyes above a stubby little nose, a small rosebud mouth and a sharp, pointed chin. She looked like a stubborn, willful old child with a bad haircut.

She wore a forest green tunic fastened with a red belt over an indigo body leotard. Tiny, welded green frogs cavorted on the oversized belt buckle. One small, red-nailed hand toyed with the ornate buckle, tracing the tiny frogs while she contemplated the Fate that brought her to such a sorry pass.

She pictured vengeful thunder rolling above the emaciated, gray robed-with no viable trims-mumbling, ornery do-gooder Fates, deafening them and producing lightning bolts striking their sorry asses, startling and confusing them while they wended their smug, purposeful way through the world, passing out whatever Fate to whomever they damn well pleased.

She glanced down at the journal, her lips trembling. She sighed. Sometimes frustration got the better of her. The moving lines on her face finally sank beneath the collar of her leotard. The ink dried up some time ago. She picked up the journal and started writing again.

She was standing at the open attic window, re-reading a page when a gust of wind grabbed it and tossed it down towards the sidewalk. She closed the shutters, lowered the window, ran downstairs, but took a minute or two, to decide between the dark blue or pink umbrella before she opened it and rushed out into the rain. She searched up and down the sidewalk and in the shrubs, but the page was gone.

Oh what the hell! How important could it be anyway? Surely no one here gives a damn about an old lady's nutty fantasies, ramblings or philosophies, she thought. She went inside and shut the door.

Chiffon is transparent, translucent, light as a feather, as light as a bevy of happy, dancing thoughts. So there you might have it!

Ćhapter 4. Blizzard's Kin

Looking like an ancient, immobile monolith, Lucian Bellsted Solestone stood planted on the sidewalk in the slanting rain, an inscrutable expression on his swarthy face. Tall and spare in his black raincoat, with no umbrella or hat, his stance was that of a pirate standing on a ship's deck in a storm. His thick black hair air lay in silver-white wings at his temples. The people walking past him gave furtive glances at his frowning, chiseled mouth, hawk nose and heavy black brows, then hurried on their way. He ignored them, keeping his eyes fastened on the window above. He knew all about intensity, all about watching and waiting. *Til' the first of never,* he thought ruefully.

He watched a small, curvy hand reach out and swing the blue shutters, the color of the morning sea, inward. His heart thumped madly for a second and he remembered Laine and Minnie. Lost at sea. He shrugged. Everyone suffered losses as they aged. It was a part of life. He listened to the shutters snap shut and the latch click.

He reached in his coat to touch the page he'd grabbed out of the rainy night air. It was dry and secure in an inner pocket. A thin mist swirled around the people hurrying by. Umbrellas raised, they stepped quickly around him while he stared up at the cottage window, waiting for someone to come out, but no one appeared.

Impatient at the best of times from a personality that dipped too low into the dark reaches of his soul, scouring and burning if he tarried too long over any one thought or lingered too long in any one place, he lifted his right hand to check the time. The leather banded, square faced watch rimmed with gemstone chips showed ten o'clock. He glanced at the cottage, shrugged, pulled up the hood of his raincoat and moved on.

The headlights glow from the occasional passing car outlined his substantial frame as he turned each corner slowly and deliberately. He moved steadily through the damp darkness, following the familiar route he took on his nightly constitutionals. He drew in deep, enjoyable breaths of the salty, wet air as he walked. Night was his favorite time of day any place, especially here. Deep in his own thoughts, he rarely glanced up from the wet, mirroring sidewalk.

As he turned the corner onto Main Street, the rain sluicing off the ocean slowed to a mist, softening the glow of the lights in the small tourist shops. He lifted his eyes from the wet street and let them roam the familiar shapes. He knew all of their dark surfaces; he'd walked this route since he was a young man.

He knew the shape of each shop in the village and what the whole of it looked like in any season or time of day. He knew the shop owners and their families. He knew their work habits but not much more, despite having been born in this place.

He didn't know people well. He didn't like to. He knew what the summer tourists said and bought. The thing he knew most about was Winter's Lee's sea. He knew the language this part of the sea spoke. He knew when it was tranquil, a state that never lasted long in any of the cold northern regions of the world. He watched the sea countless times from the cliff tops behind his house, reveling in the huge, dark storms his morose soul craved.

The bookshop was tucked between a grocer and a watch repair shop. Its long thin windows sent out inviting light.

He stopped to shove his hood back and rake the rain's dampness through his thick hair with his long fingers. He pulled out a large white handkerchief and mopped his face, hair, and hands dry as best he could.

He glanced through the window at Old Stanton, the owner. That elderly, white-haired gentleman was stacking books at his usual snail's pace in a corner. The bookshop was in the same building with Stanton as the owner, since Lucian was a child. The shop carried new books for tourists and a mix of vintage, rare, and hard-to-find books for other, more avid bookworms. The bookshop used to be one of his father's favorite places in the village.

Old Stanton was as predictable as rain. He had been one of his father's best friends and in the old days, the two of them shared many meals, wines and rare books together. In those days, Lucian was sometimes invited to join them in a game of chess or a discussion on rare books. Their predictable habits and solid friendship offered him solace many times. He suspected they knew of his troubled, sad soul though they never mentioned it.

He turned the doorknob and stepped inside, looked around and sniffed appreciatively. The bookshop smelled best during a rain, with aromas of dripping candle wax, learned words, and a familiar smell of print and page. He sighed. The bookshop and old Stanton were two of the few reasons he still came home.

Old Stanton turned at a snail's pace and gave him a solemn look.

"Lucian. Can I help you with anything?"

"No, thank you, Stanton. I'm just browsing tonight."

"I have those books you wanted, Lucian. They came in earlier today. Would you like them now, or would you prefer to wait until a different time? It's raining pretty hard."

"I'll come back tomorrow and pick them up. Thank you, Stanton."

Old Stanton nodded and turned back to his work. Lucian glanced around. The bookshop was empty. Stanton was nocturnal; he opened the bookshop in the afternoon. Sometimes he forgot the time and stayed past closing at eleven.

Lucian browsed casually through the popular book titles as he edged towards the back of the shop. He stopped between two bookshelves and glanced around before he took the page out of his pocket.

I didn't knock on the cottage door because I wanted to read what was on the paper, he admitted to himself. With his luck, the page probably held shallow words dripping with guilt, a grocery list, the usual missive to a mother, a lost lover, or an ex best friend. Maybe words addressed to an errant child, a world traveler who always forgot to return home, like himself.

He unfolded the page and stared at the lines written in ornate, passionate purple script. He snorted. The page looked like an overdressed chorus girl, full of frills and silliness! It couldn't possibly say anything meaningful! He almost crumpled it into a ball and threw it away. There was a waste basket near the front counter. He could toss it in on his way out. Then he stopped himself and sighed.

"What the hell? Why not?" he muttered, already disappointed and bored. He smoothed out the crumpled paper and scanned the words quickly and expertly, expecting to find no depth.

"The illustrations etched upon my body through circumstance, terror, and yes, sometimes excessive thirst, caused from those damn dippers of water I drank in the cave, no doubt loaded with something, lend their silver lineage to the lessons brought forth from my past lives for me to contend with this lifetime. Their great resonance upon my eternal being proclaim that I will meet those same- guess what names I would like to call them, but won't out of stark fear- teachers where they await my next incarnation with further lessons. But I have some fresh news for them. If I succeed this time, they won't see the backside of me again! And I hope to succeed, though I have no idea how. If I don't, there is no way out; I will remain forever Hesta at the hearth, living out a fated existence alone, scrubbing ashes into my soul, exfoliation waiting with no soothing balm or good skin cream available, having searched for and never found the love I so desperately need to companion me on my soul's journey. I grow old without respite."

What the hell is this, he wondered, snorting again as the intense, silly, needy words in their ornate purple script pranced past his defenses and came to rest near his heart. Before he knew it, they had settled in without permission, leaning against the white fencing surrounding the hidden hurts of a lifetime, waiting to see what he thought of them.

Shocked, he muttered "Squatters!" bidding them leave, thinking of Lainie and Minnie, trying to avoid the avalanche of hurt remembering them brought.

He pushed his emotions away, folded the letter and shoved it in his coat pocket. Old Stanton's back was still turned. He nodded at his back, let himself out and strode home, trying to outpace the tiny hope suddenly settled in without rights or permission near his hurts.

"They don't need a companion!" he muttered to himself.

*

He sat by the lit fireplace in his study, dignity restored. He sighed. His grief over losing Laine and Minnie somehow caused this, he reasoned. That's why the silly page bothered him.

He'd protected his heart from his parents and Melanie, never asking questions, never wanting to know more, not wondering why. Lainie changed all that. His lifelong, primitive need to defend from closeness was damaged. There was a crack in his defenses. He had danced too close to love.

He frowned down at the page in his hand. A ridiculous ballet of words dressed in purple, ruffled flounces. He huffed out a derisive breath. Why, a man shouldn't have to put up with such a silly thing! But the damage was done. The crack was breached, and he felt it deepening. The frilled, purple words had already flown by, prancing along in notes of high C and A, past his monumental mountain of insistent short sightedness, past the carefully constructed defenses of a lifetime as though they were nothing, ignoring the rock solid, hardened pride everyone else was intimidated by.

He leaned back and closed his eyes as the last scraps of the purple scrawls settled like a butterfly in his heart. Before he could stop them, run them off, with a tender, trembling finger, the loopy, silly, drooping words touched his hidden pain. In recognition, they instantly became his companion in his secret, hurt soul. Why, the silly things nestled in as though it was a place they were born to find!

*

Today I found a long, legal looking envelope in the mailbox. The kind that tells you politely that you've become "An Important Person," for some reason to someone who probably intends to collect.

The missing journal page was neatly folded inside the envelope, along with a note and a formal card with the name Lucian Bellsted Solestone. The note said he found the page and assumed it belonged to someone living in Windbay Cottage. He had taken the liberty of reading the page and the words were curiously interesting to him. He wondered if it would be convenient to meet the author. Of course, I didn't answer.

Georgette is a silken, highly twisted yarn, akin to a story everyone tells at some time or another.

Chapter 5. Mrs. Bentley

The mist parted and swirled around him in the dusk. *I had hoped for an answer,* he thought, nearing the cottage with the sea-blue shutters. He stopped beneath the giant oak tree to stare up at the dark, open window. The dim light from the street lamp outlined a woman's figure standing in it. He watched as she leaned out the window and tipped her face up to the cool, dark mist. Instinctively he stepped back into the tree's shadow. Hidden, he stood perfectly still, a tall, angular, black shadow frozen in place under the boughs of the oak tree, hoping she wouldn't notice him.

So that's who lives here, he thought. *I wonder if she's the one who wrote those silly words.*

He watched the tides of emotions rippling across the woman's upturned face like flowing water, and immediately knew the answer. She was the one.

Something moved on her arms. His eyes narrowed in concentration as he imagined he saw thin, glowing lines moving on them. It was too dark to tell exactly what he was seeing, but it looked like the lines were forming into a tiny paw and an open mouth. Startled, he jumped back. It had to be an illusion. Just his imagination!

She noticed his movement, turned her head and looked down at him. For a long moment he stared into large gray eyes hiding nothing they'd ever seen and been through in this world. He managed to hold her look, though the pain of it caused his heart to pound and moisture to work its squeaky, rusty way to the surface of his eyes. He never cried; he didn't intend to start now, especially over a stranger.

The woman blinked and came back into herself. The remnants of her thoughts tumbled from her eyes like broken window glass falling. He heard them breaking, a raining down to where he stood, of tinkling, tiny, delicate, lost sounds.

She knew he heard it too, and she beat a surprised retreat from the window. He listened to the window shut. Misty silence fell like stone around him. After a minute he came out of his frozen stance, turned on his heel and headed home. He would go no further tonight.

He shoved his hands deep into his pockets like a young schoolboy who accidentally shattered a window. A rare flush suffused his swarthy face. He was an intruder. He'd entered uninvited into the woman's private space. He'd trespassed where he had no business. He shook his head morosely at himself.

*

He sat in the library in his favorite chair, staring at the flames in the fireplace, his long legs stretched out in front of him, his fingers tented under his chin. It was a pose he often took when he was thinking out the solution to a problem.

Polished copper railings and softly lit lamps muted the glow of the richly paneled walls, wainscoting and floor of the library. Miles of bookshelves lined the walls. Books stood like soldiers behind glass doors in wood cabinets. Books lay stacked on tables. Large, buttery leather sofas with chairs in shades of clay red and yellow ochre were grouped in cozy clusters around the lofty, cavernous room. Thick, plaid throws lay over chair backs. Masculine pillows leaned in sofa corners. Soaring green ferns and other plants in enormous copper pots casually separated the areas of the vast library into cozy, private gathering places.

The tall, handsome French windows on each side of the fireplace opened out onto a wild garden Heathcliff would have envied. The property flowed past the garden back to the sturdy black metal fence guarding the edges of the rocky, barren cliffs. Far below the cliffs ran a thin strip of beach with waves forever pounding upon it. The muted sound of the surf from below kept its constant vigil in the house.

A large mahogany desk stood near the fireplace. On the top of the immense desk lay stacks of papers in neat, orderly rows. Elaborate ink pens lay beside the papers. A crystal decanter and small crystal glasses lined up like frozen soldiers on a silver tray near them.

He was thinking about the woman in the window. His thought about what large gray eyes held and what was moving on her arms. She looked soft and vulnerable. Why didn't she have the sharp nose or the thinned down, tight mouth or squinty eyes older people usually acquired as defenses from their accumulated experiences with life? Maybe she'd never experienced being socially marginalized and excluded, like most children and older people?

*

Mrs. Bentley stopped in the doorway to study the familiar lines of his face. She thought he'd have his nose buried in an old book by. Instead, he was staring into the fire, his long frame stretched out, his craggy face pensive. His expression was impassive and unreadable, as usual.

She remembered him as a three-year-old, earnestly trying to look and act just like his father. Though he'd turned out to be a mournful man, she was always glad when he came home. But his visits home were fewer and fewer since Lainie left, taking Minnie with her.

She gave a slight shake of her head to stop that train of thought, for it would lead nowhere except into pain again. She should remember her position as head housekeeper, given to her by his parents before he was born. She still held his beautiful, dark parents, Perry and Alecianna Solestone in the greatest of esteem, and their only child was like a son to her. She defended his ways to the village, though she didn't understand them herself. She was used to his cryptic, obscure, metaphysical thinking, believing that his behavior came from the books he constantly read.

Though the people in the village sometimes wanted to know about the "strange uns" living up on the cliff, they never found out anything from her. Even her own husband and children were not able to get her to talk about the Solestones. She pushed her glasses up higher on her long nose until they covered her sharp, knowing blue eyes before shifting a long hand up to smooth a wisp of snow-white hair back into the neat bun on top of her head. She was part of this family, and she would continue to protect their secrets. That's all there was to it.

Her mouth quirked briefly in amusement. Lucian was a kind man, a man not prone to curiosity, a little short sighted, never questioning things he should, never realizing it.

He treated her as though she was a frail old lady whose hearing and sight had gone by the wayside centuries ago. He was overly solicitous and formally courteous to her and addressed her as though she needed all the help she could get. She never felt the need to confess to him that she carried a load of common sense, she was strong as a horse, and was never sick a day in her life.

Lucian liked traveling, it was in his blood, but she also knew he was a creature of habit. He had a high need for privacy, for his was an introspective nature. That's why he always came back to this huge, rambling house above the sea on top of the black cliffs. She prayed that he would always return to his home so she could tend to him.

She wondered if he brought home gemstones this time, for he'd followed in his father's footsteps. Like that of Perry Solestone, Lucian's knowledge of gemstones, antiques and rare books had secured him an enviable place in the international business world. He traveled the world, searching them out for reputable, wealthy clients.

His great need for privacy along with his inability to dissemble or question the motives of others caused him to have the reputation of being an aloof, austere man. Mrs. Bentley remembered the happy, sensitive little boy whose favorite color was blue. Later, he became a solemn young man who turned from people to books to seek solace and protection from the pain of knowing any more about the people he loved. It cost him, for there were things he didn't know and didn't want to know, but he seemed willingly to pay the price.

Because of his peculiar life stance, people often mistook him for an unfeeling man. Despite his strange, intense ways, he was slowly and steadily gaining a reputation as a humanitarian, one kind and careful with everyone he dealt with.

The few people reaping the benefits of his rare offers of friendship became loyal and abiding friends. In the beginning, each one was ready to become his enemy. Each one secretly believed he was like the northern land he came from, harsh, uncompromising, and incredibly cold. As they came to know him, however, they discovered a complex nature holding a deep well of understanding of humanity with no bitterness in it. Instead, it was cool, soothing, and accepting of their mistakes and rights and respectful of who they were.

Mrs. Bentley was well-acquainted with those aspects of his nature. He was a thoughtful, powerful child, one who grew into a thoughtful, powerful man.

His friends were scattered all over the world. He sought them out, but they rarely came to Winter's Lee. He didn't invite them, for he felt there was nothing in his part of the world to recommend itself. Mrs. Bentley would have begged to differ if her heart didn't understand him.

He turned his head and looked at her, his black eyes inscrutable. He pressed his lips together in the familiar, small smile that told her he was thinking of some remote, sad, painful, or unexplained thing. She knew he instantly noted every detail of her dress and mood, for he was well schooled in noticing the smallest details.

She touched the pin she wore at her throat. In its center was a huge blue sapphire surrounded by diamonds. The pin matched the blue of her eyes. Perry and Alecianna had given her the ornate pin for Christmas over twenty years ago.

"Do you need anything before I leave?" she asked, in the affectionate tone she reserved only for him. He shook his head no, then turned back to stare into the fireplace. Before she turned away, she studied his profile and wished he wouldn't stay so insistently and inscrutably sad.

Dimity is a lightweight, sheer cotton fabric with many uses. Many beautiful Victorian gowns were made yards and yards of it.

Chapter 6. Lainie and Minnie

He was lonely and thinking of Lainie, like he always did in the evenings. Beautiful Lainie. They'd met when he traveled to her island home in the South Pacific to assess a rare gemstone.

The trip had been arduous and long, and he was exhausted. Invited to dine at his new client's home, he sat, formal and rigid in the large, airy room waiting for the client, who was late. He sat for what seemed like an eternity in the silent room, a sad, dark, tired monolith of a man. Then Lainie waltzed through the door, and his whole world changed in an instant.

She was grace personified in her flowing, colorful island dress. He jumped up. She smiled at him. Immediately, liquid fire and warmth filled every space and surface and corner of the seaside turquoise and coral colored room. He heard the roar of the surf rushing up on the beach a few yards away—or was it the blood flowing to his expanding heart? Slim and quick, she tossed her rippling, long brown and amber hair, strode across the room and shoved the shutters open so the turquoise, carefree sea could inhabit the room with them.

Then she turned back to him, studying him openly with her black edged, golden, expressive eyes. While she studied him, his eyes traveled over thick, sun bleached, wavy hair and tanned skin. He examined her sharp little chin before moving up to her soft, pink mouth and across her short, straight nose. When he reached her strange, honey colored, waiting eyes, he was lost forever, and they both knew it.

Opposites of each other, he quickly came to crave her warmth and lightness. She, in turn, was fascinated by his monastic darkness and unspoken intensity. He fell in love so swiftly and intensely that he didn't stop to think about anything else. They married quickly, without a thought of the differences between them, and he hastily carried her warm happiness back to the cold, austere house on the black cliffs above Winter's Lee. He planned to fill the house with her light and warmth.

For a while, she smiled and sang and danced around him with ease and humor. His great frame relaxed into a sort of grace and the constant tension in his heavy-browed, deep set, somber black eyes, relaxed. His banked passion for life rose to the surface, rushing past the dark ashes he'd kept himself buried under. His soul felt freed from ancient, unknown constraints, and he began to suspect that it was possible for him to love greatly.

But while he blossomed, Lainie wilted in his cold, dark home land. Her warm nature was repulsed by the gray grimness of Winter's Lee. When she attempted to make friends with the people in the village, their naturally stoic natures damped her vitality and spontaneous warmth. She missed the colors and lightheartedness of her island home. She craved the carefree people and the precocious breezes of the southern islands filled with people like herself, people who laughed and danced and shared her values.

After a time, he realized he could not keep her in the cold northern land he called home. It was too cold and rigid for her. It was not good for her. But he needed her so badly, and it was his home, so he did everything he could to keep her there as long as possible. When she became pale and quiet, he whisked her away to other warm places for long periods of time, but never back to her island home. He was afraid she'd never leave if he took her back there, and he believed he could never live there with her.

He gave her the finest jewels money could buy, but he could not bear to let her return to her island. He didn't care if they traveled forever, he intended to keep her with him. He wrapped her in the finest furs and still she shivered. It was a tribute to the degree of her love for him that she lasted as long as she did.

Then a miracle happened. Minnie came along, and they came home to this house for her birth. Lainie stayed without complaint for a while, dancing their laughing, infant daughter through the dark, gloomy rooms in the huge house high on the black cliffs. He could still hear their laughter ringing in the air as he followed them through the rooms, turning on lights and lighting candle after candle to assure them of warmth and light.

Then the dreaded time came, as he knew it would. Lainie needed to return to her island or die. It was written in the stars, she told him. She wanted Minnie to meet her family. At the last, he accepted his fate and helped her return to her island home. He helped her take his darling Minnie with her back to her island home, where she could be warm again, where the sunlight was constant, strong, and hot. They left on a cold January day.

"Don't worry, I'll come back soon."

She whispered the painful lie to him, clutching Minnie's hand in her own, both grownups knowing it was a lie. She held up the two ship tickets and smiled. She whispered, "I love you!" before she danced away, taking the beautiful, fiery, graceful Minnie with the liquid doe eyes, rippling hair and pointed, dimpled chin with her.

He knew she was speaking the truth when she said she loved him. He felt heroic and self-sacrificing for a few days after they left, for he had decided to visit her there and try to stay.

Then he received the terrible news that their ship had gone down in a storm at sea. The ship owners and officials solemnly informed him that a few people may have gotten away in the missing life boats. He waited and prayed for Lainie and Minnie to be among the survivors, but none of the life boats were ever recovered.

While he waited, the ebony hair at his temples turned to silver. As time passed, the silver wings came to mark the beginning of his terrible, endless grief. Mercury, the messenger of the gods, had marked him with his wings. Every time he looked in a mirror, he remembered.

He would always grieve Lainie and Minnie; In the beginning, the grief almost killed him. But he survived, and after he didn't hurt so much, he looked at Mercury's mark on him with acceptance. The silver wings carried a message from the Fates that he was to remember each time he looked in the mirror. He was to never forget that love never deepened or lasted with him. He never trusted himself with loving another woman again.

A small chunk of wood fell into the flames. The sound of the tumble and collision of sparks broke into his dismal thoughts. With relief, he turned his mind to the odd woman in the window. He recalled the world he'd glimpsed in her gray eyes. That fleeting moment caught him off guard. It usually took years of work to get a glimpse of another person's soul, but he'd simply looked up, and there she stood. An old dreamer standing in an open window at dusk. She was small, her short hair a bright, impossible orange color that surely came out of a bottle. Certainly, it was a color he'd never seen before.

He frowned. How could anyone with bright orange hair write use purple ink and ornate calligraphy so disarmingly? Surely it was too ridiculous to contemplate! Parrot Clan? He'd read something about them somewhere.

He recalled the sharp little chin beneath a small bow mouth. No doubt she was extremely stubborn and bossy. He sighed and settled deeper into his huge, soft chair. The fire danced in the fireplace. The mist outside the French windows steadied into a downpour. His eyelids grew heavy and slid shut.

He woke early and left the house. He walked the wet streets with a frown on his face. Infernal sadness had plagued his dreams all night. He'd spent the night sighing, a thing he hated doing, all because of a colorful, possibly

Parrot Clan woman and Laine and Minnie. He strolled through the outdoor market, absently looking at things. He decided to visit Melanie. His mood brightened. He'd find something for her, a special spoon or spice or something. But first, coffee and breakfast in the market. By the time he got there, Melanie would be up and out in her gardens. He strolled towards the coffee shop, filled with new purpose.

Dobby is a woven fabric characterized by small geometric patterns and extra textures. As everyone knows, mysteries are made of these.

Chapter 7. Dreamers Meeting

I wore a new sea-blue tunic to the village early this morning. There were just a few people out. I was strolling along when I caught the eye of an old woman tending a vegetable stand. She stopped sorting vegetables and stared at me.

I sighed and muttered to myself, *what's new?*

She looked me up and down. What caught her eye? My new tunic worn over a blue leotard with leggy cranes at the neck, wrists, and ankles? My silver flats or purse? My freshly colored hair or extra mascara? After a minute, with a muffled laugh, she shook a finger at me.

"You need to see Melanie Snow Rosethorn. She'll straighten you out!"

The name sounded like something out of a lurid romance novel. Was there a reclusive novelist hidden deep in the frosty, clammy, roaring rime of this place?

"Who's she?" I asked pertly.

"Oh, just a woman you need to meet!" she answered.

"I don't think so," I replied smartly.

"Believe me, as much as water needs salt to make brine, you need to meet her!" she retorted, turning her back to me with finality.

Suddenly my bravado emptied out. I backed away from the old woman's loud voice, turned and walked quickly through the crowd of tourists beginning to gather around us.

I hurried through the door of Windbay Cottage and locked it behind me. I tossed my oversized silver purse on a low table, pulled off my shoes and sat down in the living room. I waited, still as a stone, for my faithful, daily dose of depression and sadness to overwhelm me.

I was odd, with an almost desperate need for both privacy and creativity. I couldn't begin to explain myself to myself, much less to others. I tried to stay in what people labeled a "positive" mood, but sometimes it just wore me out.

Oh to hell with it! I muttered. I decided to take a nap. I changed into a pair of baggy sweat pants, pulled on a sweatshirt and climbed into bed with my bunny slippers on. I wiggled them and smiled. I wore them when I needed companionship. I could just wiggle my toes, a simple activity, look at them and feel better.

I owned a restless, curious nature, so while I innocently napped, my nosy, busybody unconscious or whatever, kept the name Melanie Snow Rosethorn running through my mind like a readout on a ticker tape. When I woke up, I knew I would seek her out and no doubt get myself into more trouble.

Craftily, I waited until the vegetable market was closing before arriving again, demure in black this time, to ask the vendors about her. All they would tell me was she was born in Winter's Lee. They are a close mouthed bunch. That's one of the reasons I chose this place, although their reticence doesn't always work in my favor.

"Her place. Tarryton House. Down that way. All by itself. Not far." an old man at last divulged, his gnarled finger pointing down the beach. He ruminated on whether to tell me more, but decided against it. I was on my own.

I set out the next afternoon to find Tarryton House. I tried to look like I was just out strolling for exercise. As soon as the village was out of sight, I tromped purposefully down the narrow trail leading between sand and rocks. Stands of scrub trees and dunes stood between the trail and the beach. I couldn't see the sea, but I could hear the roar of waves.

I trudged along, came to a sand dune, climbed it, and looked around. I shaded my eyes with my hand and soon spotted a huge, white wood confection resembling a giant crooked white wedding cake off in the distance. I studied it. Was it Tarryton House? It had to be. Else what was it? Then I remembered the huge house towering above the black cliffs the first day I arrived. This one sat perilously close to the edge of the ocean too, a mysterious towering monolith partially hidden behind a thicket of trees.

I shuddered and made my way towards a random path that looked like it ended near the architecturally random house. I crossed acres of skimpy, sand choked grass under occasional shade trees interspersed with statuary and fountains. Everything looked tossed around by a careless child. Thick rows of trees and bushes were planted hit or miss, probably to provide protection from the wind, maybe to give privacy from prying eyes. A long line of restless, white-topped waves murmured in a surly, straight row beyond the enormous confection.

I stopped near the huge white object and stared up and up, until I staggered backwards. *Four stories high? Maybe five?* I aimed towards the side of the house, admiring the intricate nautical scenes carved on the window shutters.

I stepped over shells and driftwood borne up from the sea and came to a rickety gate. I stepped back and studied the line of sand holding the gate firmly shut. This trip was turning into an endurance contest.

I decided to climb over the fence, even though I was wearing a pink leotard accented with beads at the wrists, throat and ankles, and a lavender tunic with frog green ruffles on the hem.

Out of respect for the unknown Ms. Rosethorn's possible reaction, I had toned my outfit down by adding a simple matching pink leather purse, belt, and sandals. About half way over the fence, I realized sandals may not have been a good choice for this adventure. But who knew it would take an extended journey across a sandy desert loaded with obstacles just to get to this huge, sideways stack of a house?

I half fell from the fence onto the sand on the other side of the gate. I picked myself up, brushed my clothes off, emptied the sand out of my sandals, then surged forward, aiming for the central regions of the path not covered with small sand dunes.

I was half convinced the wide white porch was a mirage by the time I reached the steps. I hiked up at least a dozen steps and traversed an incalculable width of porch before at last, mercifully, I reached the door. But it wasn't over yet. I was forced to wrestle a large pot of ivy aside before I could ring the doorbell.

I pressed the button, then leaned against the door jamb, sweaty and breathless. The porch looked deserted. Sand deckled the corners, and there were no chairs to sit on. Even though certain death is guaranteed to any plant I try to grow, I could tell that the overgrown ivy in the pot I shoved aside had not been watered or trimmed in ages.

After a long wait, the door opened. A large, handsome woman stood looking down at me, her face a study in wonder. I looked up at her and grinned.

She was in her early sixties, sort of like I might be. Tall, dark, and weighty, her shiny black eyes held secrets. A thick black and silver braid hung across her shoulder to her waist. Crow's feet lined her eyes and furrowed a square, strong chin. Because she was so beautiful, I allowed my eyes to travel over her face. High, wide cheek bones, a straight nose above a wide mouth. I met her eyes. In them stood ageless learning. I was meeting an old soul.

"Everyone else uses the front door," she said, interrupting my musings. She shoved on the screen door until it opened a crack.

"Can you make it through there?"

I squeezed through the small opening and followed her down a long corridor leading into a large, pleasant room. She motioned to an ocean of sofa. I rushed it and perched dutifully on a corner cushion. She didn't ask if I liked tea or wanted any. She simply said, "I'll make tea." and left.

This woman bore the same regal bearing as the Shaman women on the island. Suddenly I wanted to forget I ever heard of this place or her, and leave Winters Lee on the next available raft, pontoon, plane, whatever, no matter how small or large. If it was small, I could wear a life jacket, because I couldn't swim. Preferably one in lime green-that coddled my sense of safety. I envisioned luggage packed, racing for parts unknown to her or the Fates, while praying mightily to whichever gods might be listening- snoopers - to spare me from any further trouble!

I looked around nervously, checking for ropes, chains, racks or torture devices, anything indicating I was in for yet another initiation.

A piano was angled into a sunny corner. Sunshine poured through windows. Enormous green plants and long, overflowing shelves of books were everywhere. Big thick squares of soft, colorful rugs dotted shiny wood floors. The vast, overstuffed sofa I perched on matched the green and yellow curtains on the windows behind the piano.

Cats napped about the immense room. They lounged large and long and lean, six of them in black, white or butterscotch, dangling paws off bookshelves and chairs as though they owned the place.

She returned carrying an ornate silver service. She poured tea for us. I was flushed and thirsty from my earlier exertions. I drank noisily then swiped the sleeve of my leotard across my face. The tea was delicious.

"This thing is just too damn hot!" I complained. I darted a quick look at her. She merely sipped her tea, looked at me and waited. I fumbled and picked at my clothes, alternately fluffing and crushing the tiny purple walrus perched atop my satin covered pink belt buckle. After a long silence, I realized she wasn't going to speak first. It was up to me. I stared out a window and shrugged like it didn't matter.

"A woman at the market in the village said I needed to see you."

My heart was pounding.

"And you are...?

"Avalon Blue."

I watched her hide her mouth behind her hand again.

"A name as extraordinary as your looks," she finally said politely.

"What is it you want, Avalon Blue?"

"You are Melanie Snow Rosethorn? They said you could tell a person's future. Oh, I don't know!"

"Yes, I'm her."

The silence thickened and spun forward. It became a living blanket, wrapping me in golden silence. I listened to her words from a peaceful distance.

"A woman your age out on quest and in your state of being is unpredictable. You don't have the usual desires most women have because of that. That leaves me in a doubtful position as to predicting your future."

She laughed, showing large, perfect white teeth. I shuddered at her words, spontaneously running my hands over my arms and chest.

"I'm living with it as best I can, every day."

She nodded. She was finished. We spoke of the weather and the village and finished our tea. She stood up and invited me to visit again. It was time to leave.

Lame' is available in unusual varieties, sometimes even eccentric, depending on the composition of the threads in the fabric. So are people.

Çhapter 8.   Lucian and Melanie

Melanie and I were born within a day of each other during a winter storm that besieged the village for three days. Empty boats sank in the cove beneath the black cliffs. Fogs and mysterious mists rolled in and covered the shoreline and the village. Lightning struck the old church by the graveyard two days in a row, finally toppling the church steeple.

Christmas was just past, a New Year ready to begin. No one was hurt, for these are canny folks when it comes to weather. Our parents replaced the steeple and boats and soothed the mystery of our entry into the world with money and dry words of ancient wisdom.

Our parents told us the stories, laughing at the solemn demeanors and too serious natures that came with the sign we were born under. We always wondered if the stories were true. The village storytellers always swore they were.

Our family's relatives lived worlds away from this northern fishing village. Melanie's family moved here first; mine followed. They had their reasons; we assumed it was a need for privacy. Each of us was an only child. Our laughing, affectionate parents got together and traded stories about us. They were delighted with us and found our prim, staid ways amusing. They laughed ruefully over the memories of how was to have raised a baby, then a child who watched them with quiet stares of disapproval when they didn't get their parenting duties right. Both our families agreed that we were old souls. We were, are, and always will be, inseparable best friends.

Our first five years passed in a joy of learning through dance, different languages, and being included in our parents' intellectual pursuits while watching their endless flow of love for each other. The time passed too quickly, and soon it came time for us to matriculate at the village school.

We dressed in somber black for our first day. It was the only color we were willing to wear to the dreary school lurking below our beloved black cliffs. We sneaked into the school earlier in the summer to look it over; we found it to be singularly lacking in charm, intelligence, or anything else interesting.

Even by that early age, our parents knew there was no changing either of us once we set our minds on something, so they gave in. Hence we were allowed to wear black to school. We passed wearily through the sanctified halls of higher learning, the other children whispering behind our backs.

Instead of playing with them, we ignored their silliness and games. We spent our extra time browsing through the neglected cemetery behind the ancient, twice-lightning struck-church on the edge of the village. We read the epitaphs on the moldering gravestones and made up dark stories about the people sleeping beneath the grass.

Melanie and I were nine when my father's mother, grandmother Diki Lala Bo came to visit us. She insisted that Melanie and I call her Diki Lala. We loved her instantly and stuck to her like sand burrs. We pestered her the entire time she was here.

She was almost ninety. We thought she was beautiful. She ate a lot of garlic and her hair hung down her back in a thick white braid. A heavy mustache shadowed her upper lip and large, protruding moles with hair springing stiffly from them resided on her face and arms. Her skin looked and felt like wrinkled leather. We were fascinated with her age and kept asking questions about how she got there, like it was a land she was visiting. She allowed us to feel her wrinkled face, look in her mouth and stroke her hair. We wanted to rub her feet and hold her hands but her violent overuse of too much personal sachet may have saved her

from too much fondling, as the clinging smell
of it put us off a bit.

In self-defense, I am now sure, she told us
rambling stories filled with mysterious
meanings. When she ran out of stories about
the old people she knew, we took over. We felt
it only right that we spell her with our stories
so she wouldn't wear herself out. After all, we
now knew plenty about everyone she ever met,
and where they were buried in the old country
by county, district, and name.

We made up stories from the epitaphs on
the tombstones in the cemetery. We knew our
stories helped her to sleep better; she
frequently fell asleep when we were telling
them.

She smelled musty and powdery, like an old
baby. We wanted to sleep with her, but she
wouldn't let us. She said she walked in her
sleep and snored too loud. We sneaked into
her room almost every morning and watched to
see if was true. Sometimes she woke up and
caught us and threw the black shoe she kept
at the ready at us. We considered the snoring
and noises she made while sleeping as an act
of relating to us from the unseen side of life.

Best of all, we loved the way her wrinkled
skin felt when we rubbed her. We counted the
moles and odd hairs growing on her arms and
face. We loved her skin like most people love

the skin of newborn babies. In other words, we couldn't keep our hands off her.

She stayed for months. We grew close during her extended visit. She taught us dances and how to light a fire in the dark. We learned how to clap our hands and hold our heads properly. We hoped she would never leave. When she went home, we never saw her again. She was too old to make another trip from the Old Country.

We were absolutely bereft. We needed more. We were off to a fine start with grandmother Diki Lala Bo, so we searched out the old people in the village. We hit on a gold mine. The village was chock full of old folks willing to let us care for them. We ran errands, combed hair and were spellbound by their stories, which usually involved catching magic fish or stone crabbing. It was the way they told them, you see.

We held their hands, smoothed their faces, and heated bowls of soup. We counted ear hairs, (thirty-seven was the average for the men, twenty-three for the ladies), and carried their slippers. Many of the old people spent a lot of their time on the other side, like naughty children playing in a forbidden-as yet-playground, leaving their bodies behind to be tended to.

The children in the village played sports and games, avoiding anyone older than themselves like the plague. They thought we were nuts, and shut us firmly out of their world. We didn't miss that world until we were older and needed friends. We were too busy with aged people, tombstones, old books, anything with dust on it, to miss other children.

*

Our friendship has lasted these many years. It has stayed steady through Melanie's marriage that began years ago, and my marriage that didn't last long enough to count.

Melanie's large brood grew up and moved away, but I still remember the huge, happy house on the outskirts of the village. It was a house full of all ages and sizes of children and Melanie's absent-minded professor husband.

Filled with sensibility and affection for him, keeping in mind that her biological clock was ticking, Melanie set aside the need to find the passion a part of her was searching for, and married the old professor.

Melanie and Abe bought Tarryton House for a song, right after their honeymoon. Empty for years, no one else would buy it because it was haunted. It was haunted then and still is.

A great white elephant of a place, Tarryton House sits out on a sand point below the village. It was one of the first houses built in this area. It was fully-documented that an affluent ship builder first owned and occupied the house, so the historical society wanted to put a picture of it on the tourist brochure. Melanie refused. She told them she wasn't going to put up with tourists. Besides, Tarryton House was still haunted, and would scare them off.

Melanie and Abe settled happily into the huge, rambling place. It suited them perfectly. The house gave Melanie the space she needed, and the old professor could wander around freely.

They didn't cut trees and trim the years of overgrown shrubs back like the village expected. They left everything to grow wild, and eventually it formed a living screen that effectively hid their large family from the view of curious tourists strolling up and down the narrow, dusty beach path near their compound.

Their children filled the house and grounds with laughter and noise. Over time, rope swings and tree houses appeared. Tunnels wove themselves in and out of the shrubs. Worn paths led across the yard down to the beach. Happy voices filled the house, yard and gardens. Melanie contentedly gardened and cooked. She first tended babies, then walking, running, laughing children.

Melanie hired Megan Watts, a widowed village woman, to help keep order amidst the chaos; to see to it the things needing doing got done. The children nicknamed Megan "Wattie." "Wattie" was old, cranky, and superstitious. She shivered over the ghost stories the children told her. She would only come to the house during the day.

The children grew up highly educated in old traditions and rife with new ideas. When they complained to Melanie about Wattie's crankiness, Melanie told them they needed her in their lives to offset their own happiness. When Wattie grew too old and sick to work, Melanie moved her into Tarryton House and took care of her. The children pulled pranks on her, just as always. Wattie complained they would be the death of her before her time. She called them little rogues, and said she was tired of them saying they were doing it so she couldn't say she was dying of boredom. They saved graham crackers and sneaked glasses of rum and ginger ale into her room, leaving them on her bedside table. She wasn't with them long before she passed away. The children grieved her as though she was their grandmother.

Melanie and Abe entertained visitors from all over the world. The visitors spent time cooking at in the big kitchen or out on the grills. They told fascinating stories, for both Abe and Melanie were skilled at bringing out the best in people. Some of their guests liked to experiment with recipes so there were always mysterious boxes filled with herbs and unusual food items delivered to their door.

Melanie invited me to dine any time I wanted to, and I went, for she alone understood how isolated I was after I lost Lainie and Minnie. Professor Abe was steadily and distantly friendly. It was all part and parcel of life. We were content with it.

Their numerous children grew up and moved away, though they migrate home for Christmas each year. Then Abe passed away. When Melanie and I get together now, it's just the two of us and sometimes her friend Bart.

Adhesive pads made from moleskin fabric can be stuck to the skin to prevent blisters, while groundhog skin reduces swelling.

Chapter 9. The Groundhog and the Mole

I glanced at the clock and laid the journal down. It was time to dress for tea at Melanie's. I decided to wear a pale blue tunic over a deep green leotard with sparkling water reeds bordering the ankles, wrists and neck. I added a pair of dark blue walking shoes with tiny scenes of water reeds painted on them. At the last minute, I wrapped a long, thin, pale blue scarf around my neck. But none of my ingenious preparations did any good.

I started out fine. I crossed the gritty sand dunes with purpose, sailing around the house to the front door. I rang the bell and stood back, squaring my stance, leaving my oversized black sunglasses on. My thin blue scarf snapped in the sea breeze, and my tunic was hanging perfectly. I felt confident and in control. At least I had the right door this time.

Melanie opened the door. I grinned up at her. She looked me up and down. It didn't take her long because I am short. She put the back of her hand over her mouth again like the first time we met. She opened the screen door. It creaked noisily, causing me to jump. It sounded like the door to my cabin on the island from hell. Fear and old memories of the animal tattoos I received while on the island flooded me.

I followed Melanie into the house. She motioned me to the sofa and left to make tea. I sat in silence, remembering how my current nomadic existence came about.

The Mole that Loved the Darkness

I was called out into the world to be brave, to live and stay in the light, but it was a foreign place to me. I held onto my children, my man and my friends so I could stay above ground. I hoped it would last all my life, but it didn't. My spirit and soul wouldn't let me pretend forever; they had other plans for me.

My husband and job disappeared. I wasn't able to be the good mother and good wife, the kind who dies with a scratch and sniff epitaph smelling like sugar cookies, one that reads something like, "Trusted and devoted mother, wife and grandmother." No, my Shadow had tried to claim me many times, though I fought it despairingly, knowing it would win in the end. I put up a good fight for many years before I was forced to descend into the darkness. I tried desperately to keep all the rules that dwelling in life above ground requires. Disguised as a human being, I scratched for gold in the light above ground complaining like everybody else. I felt like a fake, and I was. But it made me a part of them, and I wanted to keep that so badly I didn't mind being an imposter.

Somehow, I knew the light was a gift only as long as I could stay in it. I knew I was rich, oh, so very rich, when I was in it! I managed to stay in the light for a long time, but the Shadow stalking me grew longer and heavier. It called out to me and followed me relentlessly. In the end, I was forced to give in. I gradually became sad and hostile to my environment.

Deep down, I began to admit I had never been where I was supposed to be. I was living a lie. I was supposed to be shunned and alone forever. I was a dark traveler in disguise, born to go down into silent, black shades of darkness and stay there.

In the beginning, when I was young, both the Groundhog and the Mole claimed me through dreams with their peculiar ways. Their claims on me grew steadily stronger over the years and by middle age, my guts and blood and hormones were changing, bringing me ever closer to the waiting darkness they dwelt in. I cried out in anger and rage and fear, but it did not stop the inevitable. I fought it with all I was, but inexorably, I sank down into the darkness. Shorn of my resistance, mocked into ashes by my Shadow self, forced to leave my Beloveds above ground, I became a dweller in a deep, dark hole.

The Fates I fought for so long were kind. They gave me the gift of time above ground, and it was good. Now that time was over. I lost, and I would keep losing the many kinds of loves that only Light brings.

My Beloveds swayed high above me on solid ground in the light, dancing in bursts of indignation and anger over my betrayal, wailing over the shattered image of who they thought I was. I left my heart with them. It was all I had to give, and it shattered into shards so I could leave it there. They turned from me. They couldn't trust me anymore. In the doing of that, they helped separate me from all I had known and loved above ground.

Bitterly, I realized that Spirit alone could understand me now, in this dark place below. What a bitter job my children and I had, me being their mother, and they having me for a mother! And yet we had danced together and laughed together and grown strong together up in that light! I succeeded in some things and utterly failed in others.

I had reached the bottom of my life and knew it. I lived and walked alone, and it felt like I was where I was supposed to have been all my life. Once in a while, I made a feeble attempt to go back up into the light, to see them, to get on a plane and fly to my Beloveds, but I couldn't do it.

For a long time, I wanted to die, but I didn't know how. I grew more solemn and older and older. Time passed. The place I dwelt in grew deeper and darker. At last, I came to understand that the only way I could live at all was to give up the last little bit of myself, to surrender to the darkness below and forget about the Light above. I had to be shriven by Spirit, for Spirit contains both the light and the dark; hidden in the spiritual darkness might be the keys to my lost self.

And so I began my journey. The memories of the Light and what lived high above began dimming. So I could live, I began to dig down. I dug and dug and dug, claws and fur covering me, the only things I had left. My words became grunts and my mouth pink and small. My tongue became long and thin, needing protection and water. I wanted to survive. I lived hungrily and mindlessly in a void full of echoes. I dwelt in a dark, far away land that knew no sun and held no time. I fell deeper into the darkness, and still I stopped once in a while and stared up at the top of the hole, paws and guts quivering with hope. With blind eyes, I searched for the rays of light to come down into the pit and find me, to touch me, to love me again, but they never did.

Sometimes I dwelt in faraway places. When I moved on, they did not exist anymore. I left them without a backward glance. At last a time came when I stopped looking up towards the light. I couldn't look up any more; I had to look down. I let go of my children's cries to come back. I looked away from the hands held out to me. I looked down into the night that covered me, and wearily turned down into it.

I began to search through the soft, heavy darkness. It was a darkness filled with nothing, and after a time, I accepted it as my companion. I began to make travel tunnels in it. Silence surrounded me in my cathedral of darkness. I began to sense that there were many forms, figures, and layers to darkness. Some hollow, some soft, some filled with harsh, brittle, hard meanings never to be spoken.

As I dug deeper into the earth, I became primitive and fond of myself. All I thought about was food, warmth, and sleeping. When I found them, I took them. I didn't want the light any longer. It was too harsh and it blinded me when I surfaced. It hurt too much.

The Groundhog that Saw the Light

Once or twice a year, I was let out into the Light. I don't know by whose hand or will, or how it came to be. I filled that precious time with connection as fast as I could. I called my children and seized any possible way to see them. In those times, I wanted the old ways back. I hunted and searched and bargained for them. I was driven in my endless search, but it was impossible. A flood of time was passing me by.

There was never enough time before the Great Mother's Moon overrode me again, pulling me back down into the darkness, where I grieved and raged and yearned with all the ragged remnants of what was left of my human heart and soul for the past I left behind, for the *once upon a time* when I was human.

The time came when I couldn't pretend any longer to be something I wasn't, even above ground. I couldn't stay in touch with my children, friends, or relatives. I became silent above the ground and searched for food and shelter like I did down in the darkness.

During those times above ground, Light made motion of me. Light took me over with consent from Spirit. I knelt in sanctuaries to pray and drove through silent, starry nights to desert places. I took mineral baths. For hours and days, I drove and drove, searching, but for what I did not know. I fled through black nights, car windows rolled down, old rock and roll blasting on the radio, drinking caffeine free sodas, chain-smoking cigarettes. The air blew across my arms, cooling them. The wind whipped through my hair and sometimes I could swear somebody rode in the seat beside me.

I looked up at the starry skies while I drove. Somewhere across the constellations lay another land, a better place to be. I was a speck of nothing, completely alone, a tiny life moving between stars and rain and the earth and sky, going nowhere, being nothing.

In those times, the only thing I trusted was the warm, dark smallness of my fur and paws. It was all I had left, and when I flung it off, it sat and lay and rode beside me, a silent companion wherever I went, keeping track of my lost humanity.

I watched motels flash by the windows. Off in the distance lay the promised land, but each time I got there, I had to pass it by. I could not stop, for the Groundhog and the Mole had to have the darkness to survive.

*

A rattle of dishes from Melanie's kitchen broke the spell I was under. I remembered where I was. I sucked in my breath and waited. The lines fled below my collar just as Melanie came in carrying a tea tray.

"It's okay," she said soothingly. "All we need to do this moment is drink our tea."

She poured the fragrant tea into cups.

"Jasmine tea?" I guessed.

"Partly. It's jasmine mixed with orange blossoms."

"I see." I couldn't think of anything else to say. Melanie studied me thoughtfully with her knowledgeable eyes.

"Do you like gardens?"

"Yes."

"I suppose you have a green thumb?"

"Actually, any plant I go near seems guaranteed of a swift, certain death."

Melanie laughed.

"Would you like to work with me in my gardens?"

"Aren't you afraid I will kill your plants?"

"No." She didn't explain any further. I shrugged. I nodded a mute yes.

Flannel remains a sturdy cloth, useful for any kind of winter weather.

Chapter 10. The Groundhog and the Mole in the Garden

Melanie is teaching me about planting. I go over in the mornings and work in the garden or wander up and down the beach collecting sea shells. Sometimes she leaves me and goes to tend an errand in the house or village. But she always shows up when I need to be taught something.

I like this digging in the ground. The Groundhog and the Mole like resting above ground in the light with no one around. Sometimes, when she is gone, I lay down on the rich, dark dirt.

I have new leotards made of the lightest weight summer materials, but they are still too warm in this northern summer sun. I guess Hell has a suitcase and likes to travel too. If Melanie ever asks about them, I plan to explain that I have a skin condition and can't bear the sun on it.

Sometimes I watch her when we're working. She is a silver haired dark faced, hallowed presence edging closer to me. I yearn to tell her everything, to spill my guts to her. I find myself tossing bits and pieces of information to her. The more she knows, the better I feel.

*

The need to tell Melanie everything grew too strong, until it finally burst loose one day in her garden. I had decided to go to Melanie's and work in the garden even though a storm was coming in. I felt weighty, dense, and mean with the distinct possibility of becoming monstrous, just like the storm. I had to get out of Windbay Cottage.

The roar of the sullen waves breaking on the beach behind Tarryton House was pleasing. I stomped around the back of Melanie's house and out to the garden. Melanie was there, no hat, her hair in a braid. She looked up and smiled at me, then went back to work. It was just as well. I had learned a few extra cusswords during several of my initiations that her virgin ears might not like to hear!

I scowled, then fell to my knees and went to weeding. We both worked steadily. The sky grew darker and the wind blew harder. I tossed a weed up into the wind. I didn't give a damn if it landed on Mars. Melanie stood up. She pressed her hands to her lower back. The roar of the ocean was louder. She pointed to the sea and said, "Look! That storm's coming in fast!

It's going to rain hard, and soon! Let's get to the house!"

I barely heard her shout over the roar of the wind and waves. I sneered at the sea. Whatever. I wasn't going to stop weeding. Nothing could make me, either. I didn't give a damn what any other living thing was doing, including the screwed up universe.

I didn't care what God's opinion was, or what else He thought He could make me do! Stow it, shove it, whatever! The sea could take a hike, take a long walk off a short pier, float to another planet, dive bomb the galaxy for all I cared!

I grudgingly struggled to my feet and glared at the menacing bank of dark, heavy clouds rushing towards us. I planted my feet apart and shook my fist at the storm. Melanie turned towards the house. I tried to turn too, but my feet seemed to be stuck in the garden soil. I couldn't leave the garden and no one was going to make me!

"By God, nothing is ever going to do this to me again!"

The shout flew from my mouth and into the wind. I was rooted where I stood. I glared at the storm with more anger than I ever felt in my life.

"You are never, ever, going to make me go through something like that again! You bully! You'll have to kill me first!"

I had no idea what the hell I was shouting about, but it felt good. I shook my fist and jeered at the dark bank of rushing clouds almost upon us. Defiantly, I ignored the storm and fell back to my knees and started weeding as though the existence of the world depended on me getting those weeds pulled. I didn't care if Melanie was still there or not, and I didn't look up to find out. I hoped she went to the house. I didn't want her trying to change my mind. I wasn't budging from this spot. This place. Right here. Right now. No more. No more! No more!

I gasped in relief at the freedom of openly digging above ground instead of down in the dark. No more hiding. I was digging above ground, and nobody better try and stop me! I was crazy in many ways, and it was about time someone knew the full extent of it!

A thick curtain of rain came in fast and hard, pelting my back and head, shutting out the world. I was glad, relieved to give up the burden. The dirt on my hands quickly turned to slick mud. The rain stinging my back and the wind gusting and shoving on my sides were all there was in the world. I was soaked in it. A heavy muscled strength and a dark, clean peace poured through me. I laughed and clawed my hands deep into the wet ground while the wind and rain pounded me. I opened my mouth, and sounds that had been caged down in the darkness inside of me for centuries rushed out.

The storm grabbed the sounds and hurled them through the air like little itty bitty old feathers, letting me know they weren't near as weighty as I had always believed they were.

Whatever I wanted to dish out, the storm seemed to say, it could take it. It was strong enough. It was a lot bigger, tougher, and far more powerful than I ever would be, including those special cuss words I knew. The universe through which I was born into flesh was bigger and tougher than me, too.

The wind shoved me and I grabbed for purchase. My hands sought the purchase I had bought and more than paid for. I laughed. My hands clawed for deep, strong roots while the rain and lightning stormed around me. I jerked on roots. As they tore loose, I threw them as far as I could, then searched for more. A thought flashed through my mind. If I threw all the roots out, there would be nothing left to hold onto in this world. Then I could leave and be gone with the storm. Good! I didn't want anything holding me back!

I didn't realize the Groundhog and the Mole had clawed their way to the surface until I felt their lines moving and glowing on my skin. They had crawled out into the open. They were scared and clinging to me. Even though they were terrified, they understood every bit of what I was doing, for they were the monitors of my soul's destination in this moment. They had driven me into this garden, into this time.

The Mole was desperately trying to find an end to the everlasting darkness, amen. It had tunneled and pummeled and cried and crawled. The Groundhog looked up at the rain above with its great, almost blind eyes, and wept for all kinds of losses.

I felt the Mole and the Groundhog shaking and shuddering in the rain. They were through. They'd had enough. They wanted to go back home, back into the gentle darkness where they could stay hidden. They leaned against my skin, trying to find their way back to their safe places. Gentle little things! They couldn't understand my violence. They were just there, a little Groundhog and a little Mole, wanting to go back into the darkness, to hide away from the violent storm they were caught in.

Remorse struck me hard and I fell down on all fours. My heart broke. I sobbed for them, but I couldn't let them go home. I couldn't go through this again. I wailed and keened, and the storm I made inside forced them to stay above ground. The wind and rain poured down on them and scared them, but still they stayed with me, clinging, holding on for dear life.

I ripped up plants and mud and threw them as far as I could. I dug holes and sobbed with heartbreak and groaned from the lonely weariness I carried. Sanity had gone upside down. It felt so good to be an animal! To dig in the outer world in the sane, dark rain. A funny thought crossed my mind, and I laughed. I was giving the Mole and the Groundhog baths above ground!

I crawled on all fours out of the mud and stood up in the pouring rain. I don't know how much time had passed, but something was gone. I was empty.

Melanie stood watching me. She was soaked to the skin. I staggered into her arms, mud and all. I threw my arms around her and held on like a wild woman. She rocked me back and forth, smoothed my hair and murmured to me. I couldn't let go of her. The rain began to sluice the mud off of us. Then I felt her give a jerk. She put her mouth to my ear, and her words came at me like sharp nails.

"My lifelong best friend is coming across the yard right now to us. He likes storms. Don't be afraid of him. He won't hurt you. I have known him all my life, and he is one of us. I won't let go of you, and I couldn't stop him from this if I tried. It's time for it to happen."

Looking like silk but made of cotton and strongly sensible to wear and tear, Bengaline became fashionable in the 1880's and 1890's. Yet everyone knows nothing lasts forever.

Chapter 11.   Stormy Weather

I watched the gathering storm as I strolled toward Melanie's house. It broke when I was halfway there. I wandered along; no hurry. I was soaked in no time, but it is my nature to enjoy storms. The fiercer the better. My mother and father enjoyed them immensely too, but since Lainie and Minnie were lost in a storm at sea, I have both dreaded and loved storms.

I sought out storms after their loss. I stood in the rain and ice and snow and wind of this bitter place. Sometimes I still stand on the cliffs above the water to watch stormy shocks of water hurling waves against what can never be breached.

I strolled up the steps and knocked on Melanie's front door. No answer. She likes to watch the storms coming in off the ocean from the back porch. I headed around the back of the house and stopped dead in my tracks. Melanie and another woman stood in the garden, locked in each other's arms.

They were covered in mud. The garden looked like a wild animal was loose in it. There were deep holes everywhere. Alarm ran through me. Was Melanie hurt? I ran through the rain to them.

Melanie held the small woman's head pressed to her chest. Her face was hidden from me. Melanie stared at me with that inscrutable expression I'd seen before, the one that said I was being tested for a reason only she knew. Sometimes I passed her tests, other times I failed miserably.

I turned my attention to the woman she was holding. There was something familiar about her. I looked at Melanie again, and ran my hand over her face to brush the rain from it. Taking an instinctive liberty, I embraced both of them. The woman raised her face to me.

Prominent gray eyes stared at me from a mud-caked face. A face filled with stark truth and tender life. Thin silver lines raced across it in terrible, hilarious, beautiful living patterns.

Fascinated, a jolt of awareness ran through me. She was the woman in the window! I reached out and brushed the muddy, wispy hair back from her face, remembering the words from the page.

"The butterfly has lit in the rain," I said. She made a soft, hopeless little sound, turned to me and laid her head on my chest.

That simple sound and movement caused the secret, dormant hurts willed to me by my lost mother and father, my lost wife and daughter, and the many hurts that had forever hidden their reasons for being from me, to surface. My chest cracked open in relief. I heard the sharp, thin, brittle sound of it. At last they were free!

The woman felt like a tender bird or dove or some damn thing, nestled muddy and cool against my heart. I held her and stared out over the stormy water, finally admitting to the long nights that had begun long before Lainie left. I relived the hopeless sound of my darling wife's crying before she took our little daughter away.

Dimly, I heard shouts and bellows and sobs coming from somewhere off in the distance. I knew at last, and accepted that there would be no more children of my blood for me to love.

I heard the sounds again. They were the same sounds I heard standing alone on the decks of ships at sea in storms, when I knew I was alone forever and didn't care if I was washed overboard. After a while, the sounds slowed down and dimmed. At last I realized they came from me.

The woman's hand pushed against my chest. I bent forward and scooped her up in my arms and rushed with her through the rain to the back porch. Melanie reached around us and opened the screen door. I carried the woman inside, sat down in a rocking chair and held her. I felt fierce. She wasn't going to get away from me. She didn't seem to want to, either. Melanie disappeared somewhere.

Eventually, the intensity of my feelings dampened, and I relaxed a bit. The woman lay resting in my arms, still and quiet. I couldn't pinpoint when she stopped crying. I held her and stared out at the rain through the screen. It settled into a steady, undemanding rhythm.

Suddenly I realized what I was doing. I jumped up and stood the woman on her feet. How embarrassing! I kidnapped this muddy little woman and held her hostage on the porch in my arms for God knows how long!

Melanie came out holding two large, fluffy towels. She shoved them into our hands and motioned towards the doorway into the house. Her hair was wrapped in a towel. She looked clean and peaceful and not at all surprised. I was out here holding a strange woman hostage, while she casually showered and changed? And she let me?

"I've laid out clothes in the bathrooms for you to change into after you shower. While you shower, I'm going to wash your clothes and dry them." she said.

*

We showered and changed and met in the kitchen. Rain tapped steadily on the windows. The tea kettle was on. The kitchen was cozy.

Sandwich makings were piled on the kitchen table. Melanie set out mounds of thin sliced roast beef and ham, a loaf of crusty bread and dressings in frosty, cold jars.

"Lucian, help yourself," Melanie said. I set to making an enormous sandwich. Being both embarrassed and hungry, I needed an excuse not to talk.

*

I worked my way into the kitchen carefully, dressed in a lurid, copper colored floral dress of immense proportions. It was draped, twisted, and knotted so it wouldn't fall off. No problem. Nothing bothered me right now, not even this weird dress. I felt so good, both inside and out, after screaming my innards out in the garden and then being held by a beautiful, mature older man still loaded with male hormones that hadn't vacated his premises; I wouldn't dream of cussing over this dress. I mean, how rare was that?

However, the mountainous ruffled collar kept falling across my mouth like an out of order arm at a railroad crossing, forcing me to blow vigorously so I could breathe. The ruffled dress sleeves dangled far past my finger tips, so I was forced to wave them around to keep my balance.

I definitely didn't want the man thinking I was dancing for joy at finally being held by a virile, beautiful man. Well, he didn't know I hadn't been held since the first of forever, so what the heck! Maybe I didn't mind flailing around a bit just now. It was an action fitting the odd situation better than words. I wore a pair of large, pink, ruffled knickers under the dress. Where did she get these clothes?

I edged further into the kitchen and threw my eyes on her. Somehow, she knew I needed to stay covered up, but this was a bit much! I danced towards the table, kicking the lurid, trailing puddle of dress out of the way as I went, and sat down.

The man never took his intense black eyes off me. I couldn't stop staring back. I felt like a deer caught in headlights, but my eyes wouldn't mind me and stop staring at the man. They had a will of their own. He was beautiful, and best of all, close to my age. At last! My eyes wandered boldly over his thick, black hair, and I wondered how it would feel to run my fingers through the silvery wings at his temples. Would his hair feel as stubborn as he looked? I would sure like to know.

My eyes examined his face. He was swarthy, with a hawk nose and high cheekbones. He looked like an ancient pirate or a vampire. Absently, I noticed how his large, strong body strained against the pretty, ruffled pink housecoat he wore that didn't come close to meeting across his chest. He'd tied the sash of the ruffled housecoat into a sort of loose knot at the ends. How come everything was ruffled? And then there were the floral pajama bottoms he was wearing.

My eyes continued to roam ever more boldly over him, closely examining the ways he was wearing his odd clothing. He sat perfectly still watching me. Despite his clothing, he was definitely beautiful. I sighed wistfully. Of course, I wasn't going to let him know that. When I finished looking him over, I smirked at him and spoke over my shoulder, never taking my bold, roving eyes off him.

"Melanie, is the pretty pink robe the man is wearing made of rayon or cotton?"

She laughed, her back to me at the sink.

"Or is it hemp or lycra or silk, maybe?"

I knew about that stuff because of my leotards and tunics. I simpered at him and then burst out laughing. I laughed so hard I covered my mouth with my hand. I turned and slapped the table top with my other hand. There are many ways to let off steam.

Melanie turned from the sink where she was peeling eggs. I stared at her. She looked like an immense, stately goddess in a sort of toga thing, in shades of violent lime with odd looking palm trees painted on it.

"My daughter Shelby's," she explained, the words coming from a tall, confident palm tree complete with braids wrapped in lime leaves, speaking confidentially to us. "She's an artist." I pointed my finger at her and laughed harder. We all ended up staggering around the kitchen, hanging on to counters, laughing and pointing at each another.

*

Melanie stopped laughing and sat down. She turned to me, a sound of anticipation in her voice. Her dark eyes sparkled. She was grinning.

"Lucian Solestone, meet Avalon Blue!" she gestured grandly at the odd little woman.

I gaped at her, "What?"

She repeated the words slowly, as though she was talking to a very dense person.

"This is Avalon Blue."

She flung her arm toward the woman again, like the ringmaster of a circus. I looked at the woman, then back at Melanie. What a ridiculous name! Why, it wasn't respectable! It wasn't enough of a name to hold a person down to the ground! It sounded like some showgirls' name! Then I remembered the ornate purple, frilly, prancing writing.

"*Oh yes.*" I muttered to myself. I recovered enough to say, "*Hello,*" while Melanie smiled mightily at me. She knew exactly what I was thinking.

"Hello." Avalon Blue responded in a silvery, desolate edged voice. I looked at her, startled. *"Desolate?"* I thought. *"Maybe. But why?"*

"Avalon? No, it can't be," I muttered. I shook my head no and scowled at her. All wrong. A woman named Avalon would be smooth and tall or pale and stalky. At least tall. She would know a minimum of four of the old Celtic languages by heart and speak them easily at will. Especially in pubs. She would be dangerously mysterious, high breasted, very sophisticated in ritual and garb. She would be able to sing and would own a voice rivaling angels. She would have a river of gently flowing long dark hair, a delicately placed dimple in her curved chin, she would be immensely fertile, have many children, she would own much ancient wisdom to impart, and stay curvaceous but somehow slim-and young.

This little woman was plump and curvy and short and sort of old. Instinctively, I knew she couldn't sing. My eyes moved over the heart-shaped, sharp-chinned face, where a naive wisdom shone from her gray eyes. She looked like a wise, artless, inordinately stubborn, iridescent, timeless old waif. I studied her short, fluffy orange hair, and shook my head. Why, she barely reached my chin in the garden! How did she make me cry?

"Avalon Blue," I muttered to myself again, while the women ignored me and talked to each other. Maybe she was chronically sad or held a history of being hysterical. Maybe she changed her name for some reason. If she did, she certainly could have made a better choice.

Maybe not sad or hysterical. Maybe just hungry. I watched in admiration as she took a shark-size bite of her sandwich. But then, it was her in the garden. I looked at her hands. They were small and shapely.

I squinted and studied her aura like I did with rare gemstones. She emitted a curving, light energy, the kind sapphires give off. Compact, curving, strong willed and luminescent.

I was reminded of the painting of my mother wearing her favorite sapphires with a black dress. The high saturation of color in the sapphires she wore lent a muted glow of power. Mother had been a strong, beautiful, striking woman. The artist captured both her power and the glow of her sapphires in his rendition of her. The painting hangs in an upper hall of the house near the windows where she spent many hours watching the sea crashing below.

I have always been fascinated by sapphires, just as she was. Mother noticed my interest in them early on, and became my teacher. She taught me about corundum, the mineral sapphires are made of. I learned that a sapphire is valued according to its translucence, its high saturation of color and low brilliance.

Sapphires, in addition to corundum, are made of native alumina, or aluminum oxide. It is the hardest mineral, except for the diamond, and an excellent abrasive for materials of high tensile strength, such as steel. Sapphires are a strong gemstone for strong people. Then there are the wonderful colors! Pure transparent or translucent corundum is prized as a gem, and is named according to its color, sapphire blue or ruby red. The red corundum is almost never called sapphire, although it is a part of that family.

Mother collected oriental sapphires. She loved the purple sapphires, the oriental amethysts. The oriental emerald sapphires are green or yellow and are called topaz.

I nodded absently at the women. It was settled in my mind now. Avalon Blue, with her luminosity, was a sapphire. Blue, but darker. Something rare. She was the woman in the window, the one to whom I sent the letter asking to meet. Now she was sitting here before me, making a sandwich, a mundane occupation. I wondered if she was attracted to sapphires.

Melanie took another bite of her sandwich and sent me a huge smile of satisfaction. I looked down at my plate. My sandwich was almost gone. How did that happen?

"*It's B-L-U-E,*" Melanie said.

*

Melanie told the lovely man named Lucian my name. He stared at me without speaking. He didn't speak for so long I began to wonder if he could, or would ever speak again during this lifetime. Then he started muttering. "*Saffies!*" Then something that sounded like "*aluminum.*"

I nibbled my sandwich, sipped hot tea and watched Melanie to see what her reaction was to the man's state of being. She didn't seem to be bothered by the fact that the almost speechless, muttering man in the frilly pink bathrobe was temporarily out of order. Evidently, she didn't feel the need to interrupt him with small talk—for example did he want to be embalmed or not?

We ignored him and I nibbled my way through another sandwich, while fervently hoping neither one of them would bring up what happened in the garden. The event had been enlightening, emptying, satisfying and embarrassing. Would they try to get me locked up? Whatever happened, I was going to eat first.

Melanie stood and wandered into the living room, sat down at the piano and began to play. I followed and climbed into a corner of the sofa to listen.

The man named Lucian something or another sat down near me in a large leather chair. It looked like it belonged to him. The soothing music moved each of us farther away from the need to explain the garden incident.

None of us seemed to want explanations although we knew we were each changed because of it. This woman I barely knew and this man I never met before, were my companions in an experience beyond words.

The rain fell steadily. We let the sound of it and the music carry any need for further understanding of what had happened farther away from us.

*

We left Melanie's house and walked sedately along the drenched path leading back to the village. Lucian spoke formally of the ships that kept this little village alive, and of the differences between crabbers and fishermen. He didn't mention the garden incident.

Once he took my elbow to guide me past a pothole in the path. He talked about the weather and inconsequential things until we reached the front door of Windbay Cottage. I opened the door and rushed in, throwing a quick thank you over my shoulder.

Melanie sat at the piano in a red robe, silver and black hair rippling down her back to her waist. She felt intensely smug and thoroughly gratified. She hummed a little tune and thrummed the piano keys, an almost empty glass of red wine nearby.

She glanced out the front porch windows and laughed, remembering. When Avalon returned from the bathroom wearing her own clothes, Lucian snorted in suppressed surprise. She wore a dark green tunic over a lime green leotard trimmed with tiny, snow white egrets wading in silver water reeds on its edges. There were little purple things perched here and there on the tunic. She wore green walking shoes with water reeds painted on them. A long green scarf was wound around her neck and she held a pair of large black sunglasses in her hands.

Melanie knew that to Lucian the things on the tunic looked like insects. She whispered to him, "They are dragonflies circling before lighting on the water reeds!"

Feeling happily cruel, she pointed out the green shoes with the silver reeds. Before he could say anything, she handed them umbrellas and ushered them out the door. He followed Avalon out the door like a man in deep shock. Avalon hadn't noticed a thing.

"How big this old world is, and yet so small! No matter what, and most times against all odds, people come together at just the right times and places," Melanie announced to the cats. They stirred slightly and went back to sleep. Living with her, they were used to many things. Melanie yawned hugely, closed the piano and strolled off to bed.

Pulling a thread can lead to falling apart. Sometimes it is a necessary industry, though.

Ćhapter 12. **Sleep and Old Pasts**

I changed into a white cotton nightgown leftover from the old days and padded into the living room. The nightgown was simple and sleeveless, the neck a soft, low circle. I've missed this kind of carefree comfort. Since I left the island, I've slept in pajama pants and high-necked pajama tops with long sleeves, just in case there is an emergency at night. Well, I already had my emergency today. If there is any more ahead tonight, tough.

I grabbed the glass of stale water I left on the coffee table this morning, and drank it down.

The Groundhog and the Mole, two of my soul's teachers, came out in the open today, above ground. Now they owned a permanent place in both worlds with me. They were witnessed, sustained and validated by a beautiful woman and a dark man's own emotional release that somehow balanced everything out for both our human souls, the male and female sides, and for the souls of my two beautiful little underground friends.

The Groundhog and the Mole stood below in the darkness, looking up, yearning for daylight. They finally accepted the darkness and worked to survive so they could carry the eternal wisdom held by Darkness up into the Light. The two of them climbed out of the darkness and stood right out in the open with me.

Now I must take care of them differently. At seasonal tides, the Groundhog needs to hibernate. One of my duties will be to provide a place for it to hibernate, and to keep a place for it to stand fearlessly in the sunlight. The Groundhog's sureness in the dark, its awkwardness in the light and the way it looks must be respected and protected. The Groundhog cannot be called names or be teased or laughed at. It needs safe places and times to come out, so it can waddle awkwardly around without hesitation or trepidation.

The gentle Mole will always live in the place in me that holds the dark time that has no beginning nor end. The persevering Mole has kept that place of dark time in front of me unerringly, helping me in ways no human could. The Mole patiently and humbly tunneled through the vast, unending earth, searching through the darkness. It made itself familiar with it, then bravely made a home in it. The Mole learned where it could dig tunnels. It knew instinctively where the tunnels wouldn't cave in and trap it forever, causing it to lose its soul, which was timid in the Light, but vastly brave in the Dark. It knew where the warmest and the coldest places were in the darkness. It defined itself and ate and slept, and it would keep on digging and living for the sake of the life below and above.

The Mole learned the different textures and weights the darkness held; now it was not so verily afraid of the great ring of silence that makes up the Eternal Night any more, Amen. I would protect the mole from what the light of day's exposure could do to it, and it would forever remain a sacred companion down in the darkness.

Lucian. He had come to me in the nick of time and legitimized my emotional process with his own. Had he not, I would have eventually declared myself insane. Somebody, somewhere, knew that, and was looking out for me. For him, too.

Hours passed before I fell asleep. In the morning, I took a shower and looked at myself in the mirror. The moving, glowing lines of the Groundhog and the Mole were gone from my skin.

Silk hems may be varied from straight lines into scallops, tulips, and sometimes waves. As they say, variety lends spice to life.

Chapter 13. The Flame

She's short and incandescent, like a candle burning, an indeterminate age but older, like me. I want to touch every wrinkle around her eyes and know how she got them. I want to know where she got her funny, fuzzy orange hair. I want to know who she inherited her small hands from. I want to know about all husbands and lovers and children, everyone who has passed through her life.

Her soul felt like a companion to mine in the garden. The weird clothes? I sense a purpose behind them. They are too well-made and expensive, too well thought out and original to be an accident. He pondered the meaning of the lost air she wore like a protective mantle.

"Avalon Blue."

She put him in mind of the disguised insane, old, magnificent earth goddesses. The disowned, nomadic queens, the sacred, impudent princesses and the lost older souls disguised in confusion that roamed through most mythologies, carving and cutting and laughing their way through life. Women to fear, although he did not; he was nearly insanely curious.

He sat at his desk, trying to keep his mind on his paperwork instead of on Avalon Blue. His business was complex. He kept meticulous records and accounts, passing them directly to his solicitors. He was used to focusing on all aspects of his business at will. But today, he couldn't get his mind off of Avalon Blue—spelled B-L-U-E.

After a brief struggle, he laid the ornate, heavy pen down, pushed his chair back and sighed. *"Dunce!"* he muttered to himself. What happened yesterday? Why were they standing in the garden with mud all over them in the pouring rain? Why was she crying? He dropped his head. A flush suffused his handsome face.

"And I cried and shouted with her in the rain," he confided bitterly to himself. *"And I wouldn't let go of her on the back porch. I squeezed her too hard, and I wore a frilly pink robe."*

He shook his head at his own astounding behavior while a part of him measured the level of his daily emotional pain. It was down.

He called Melanie and invited himself over. She didn't seem surprised to hear from him. He noticed she sounded smug and knowledgeable about something. He guessed it was Avalon Blue. He assumed from past experience that she was withholding information he would have to drag out of her.

She was sitting on the front porch, innocently cracking walnuts when he got there. The sun was shining, the air warm and clear. No storms. Not even a hint of one in the sky. He took a seat and helped her for a while. He waited, but when she didn't volunteer any information, he knew he would have to drag it out of her.

"Mel, what happened yesterday before I got here?"

She stopped shelling walnuts.

"Luc, I honestly don't know. It's a mystery to me. She went wild and tore up the garden, then she grabbed me and wouldn't let go. We got a muddy little messenger flung into our arms yesterday."

In guarded surprise, she watched the red flush spread across his high, sharp cheekbones. She hadn't seen him blush like that since Lainie.

"Is she the reason you borrowed those matriarchal ritual books from me?"

She nodded.

"So, she is in some kind of spiritual trouble?"

"I think so."

They sat in silence a few minutes, taking in the implications.

"Did you notice anything unusual about her yesterday?"

He hesitated.

"Errr...She had on the damndest outfit I ever saw!"

It was the first thought that crossed his mind. Melanie laughed. "Yes, and she wears those kinds of clothes all the time. She's been helping me with the gardening. She always wears a full body leotard under a tunic, though they must get dreadfully hot. If I asked her, I'm sure she would say she has some skin condition. I suspect she has undergone something that has marked her skin—maybe tattoos."

The memory of Avalon standing in the darkened window of her cottage and the lines moving on her arms came to Lucian. He thought of the books Melanie borrowed. If what she suspected was true, maybe the Fates had already claimed Avalon B-L-U-E. He knew from experience and his studies that spirit chose who it wanted for as long as it wanted.

Melanie noted the look of dismay on his face.

"Let's give this mystery more time to play itself out. It seems there is more at stake here than I thought."

He nodded absently, not hearing. He was remembering the Mysteries he and Melanie chased as children. It was their favorite thing to do. When they were ten, they decided to find out what love meant, because the things people did and called love in the world puzzled them. It became their biggest Mystery of all.

They loved people's stories, but they wanted to hear more than just the nice parts, they wanted to hear all the words, beginning to end. People reluctantly told the two precocious children what they knew about love, leaving out the darker side of their love stories; this left both children feeling bereft with their results. None of the stories held the complete ring of truth, and if that was all there was to it, then everyone they knew was living a half-life.

Had the people they asked found a way to tell them what they considered ugly, dark, or too complex, they would have discovered that the two indigenous, ancient-souled children waiting before them, were Shamans who held the gift of natural acceptance of the darkness that lives within all things.

They would have learned further, that those children were pointing a way toward discovering the gold and mining it that lay within the secret and walled off places all people carry inside. But they were children after all, and the people they asked wanted to protect them from too much truth.

When they grew up, they searched the world for another with whom to share the unloved and mysterious. Their intensity and their natural understanding and easy acceptance of the unusual and the Dark's sacred ways scared off most people.

Their bodies ached to love someone whose nature was as sweetly dark and magnetic as their own, but they never found anyone else they could be both lovers with and share their souls.

Over time, they learned to accept the bits and pieces they found. Melanie needed children, so she married her elderly professor. He doted on her and wisely, never asked her any questions. Being the intelligent and sagacious man he was, he accepted her exactly as she was. That trait in him and his gentle goodness enabled Melanie to stay in their marriage. They thrived on each other's kinds of love and never resented each other's limits. They settled in together, and for a long time, raised their children and lived life in the huge house on the beach; it was sufficient enough to fill up the empty space she carried inside for a long time.

Melanie and Lucian traveled the world with their parents from the time they were children. Melanie began traveling again after her children flew the nest and her old husband passed away without a protest with her embracing him in their great double bed in their house by the sea.

Over the years, Melanie and Lucian changed for better and worse. She gained weight and he grew thinner. She admired great chefs while he became gentler and more reticent.

They both appreciated good books, classical music and fine wines. She collected seashells and small stones, he collected semi-precious gemstones and more books. Eventually both of them came home to the little northern village with the black-rocked coast line where they were born. Though not unhappy, there was an empty space waiting within them for the loves they'd never found.

Melanie carried the extra weight of a natural matriarch. She no longer wore her hair loose as a carefree maiden would. She pulled it back in a silver threaded braid when she worked in her gardens or studied herbs and cookbooks. When she entertained, she wore it in a neat coronet around her head. She became well known in the village for her healing potions and fortune telling.

The planes and angles in Lucian's face grew sharper. The silver wings in his black hair widened. He kept busy extending his collection of rare books, gemstones and artifacts while he and Melanie settled comfortably into their later years in Winter's Lee, both believing that life would never hold much in the way of surprises for them ever again.

They accepted it, though it was bitter to give up the soul's hope for the happy companionship it yearned for and never found. But what happened yesterday changed everything.

Melanie studied Lucian. Had the gods finally heard her prayers and deigned to answer them by throwing Avalon into his arms? She knew he would never get close to another woman except through the unexpected.

In the garden, in the rain, Avalon somehow triggered the release of the old heartaches he held onto since forever. He'd voiced them and flung them away with the storm. Fate had somehow intervened in the form of an eccentric looking, curvy little woman with orange hair and sparkling sequins, one who hurled herself like a muddy little dove, hurting and squalling, into both their arms. What would happen now?

The tufts and knots in boucle can be compared to the natural weave of life.

Chapter 14.   Bart

The tall, rangy man with thinning brown hair huddled close to the fireplace in Melanie's living room, his heavy, black-rimmed glasses perched precariously across his long, straight nose. They gave him the look of a contender for a book of the month club author

He stayed perpetually cold, so Melanie kept the fires burning for him even though it was summer. Bart was a cultural anthropologist. He spent time with Melanie whenever he could get away from his digs. He studied ancient matriarchal cultures, so he was constantly traveling to remote places to find more information about them.

Melanie never noticed Bartholomew Smyth-Willington until she overheard him talking about his work at a faculty party. A man fascinated by women and making a lifelong study of them impressed her. That he roamed the world, digging up things so he could figure women out meant he was special. She strolled over to listen. She narrowed her eyes at him speculatively and listened intently to what he was saying to the group gathered around him.

She looked him over. She was a large woman and he was bigger than her. She liked that. His eyes were kind, his manner shy, but knowledgeable and earnestly determined. Soon Bart found himself chatting with her, answering all kinds of interesting questions. From then on, it was just a matter of time before they fell in love.

Melanie was married when they met, and what was known to both of them for many years was never spoken of. Melanie smiled at him and thought ruefully that both she and Lucian had chosen lovers who needed the sun, who needed heat. She let that thought go.

"How about a picnic lunch in the sun?"

"Sounds good, Mel," Bart answered, shivering.

Later that day, they lounged in two white deck chairs near the edge of the yard where the grass bordered the sand. The sounds of the sea quickly lulled Bart to sleep, as always.

She watched the light breeze blowing through his hair. His hair was always unruly, too long and ever in need of a cut. The breeze picked up strands of its thin, brown length and snapped them smartly in the air, like her mother once snapped fresh, clean sheets in the air before she made beds. She sighed and settled back farther into her lawn chair. The sea's roar became a steady backdrop for her thoughts.

She knew Bart's nature thoroughly. She had hidden and lived with the depth of her affection for him for a long time, and she would continue as long as necessary. It was necessary until her husband passed away and the children flew the nest, but all that was a long time ago. Many years, in fact.

She glanced over at him. Bart was not a demonstrative man, but women were always after him. As much as he loved women, he was afraid to get too close to them. He was dry and distant with them all his life, keeping his romantic nature locked away inside his fearful heart. Only she saw past his cool exterior to the lonely, yearning soul beneath it.

She glanced at the moonstone ring he always wore on his third finger, right hand. He possessed big hands and long, large knuckled fingers. She sighed, unbraided her hair, and let it fall over the back of the deck chair.

For him, she would be young again. She closed her eyes and remembered how she thought about hands when she was young. In the days of youth, hands were for proud, hot, careless exploring of the world. In those days, her hands boldly touched unwrinkled bodies and held babies without hesitation. They explored love, herbs, and secrets with a touch of arrogance and reckless confidence.

Now, for most people her age, hands were for careful touching that stayed within the correct boundaries the current moral order defined for "old" people. How quickly young people forgot old age was only an instant away! If you were lucky.

She caressed his face with yearning eyes before she sighed and turned her face up to the sun. They would be leaving tomorrow morning on a long vacation. Maybe that would work.

The rarest of chenille fabrics may be found in unexpected places. Giraffes know all about this.

Chapter 15. Obsidian

Lucian stood waiting in the occult bookstore in the south end of London. The rare books the ancient store collected were discreetly stored in the spacious, climate-controlled archives in their back rooms.

Apart from the group owning the bookstore, only a few friends could access those rooms. Lucian was among that privileged group. He discovered the bookstore as a young man, and after many years, they accepted him into their inner sanctum. Occasionally they allowed him to purchase a rare book in exchange for informing them of a rare find in the gemstone marketplace.

A man came out from the back room.

"You can go in now."

Lucian spent days trying to find the information he wanted with no success. He turned the task over to the bookstore and moved on to his next task.

Something kept calling out to him since the day he met Avalon in the rain. Thinking about sapphires that day opened the doorway. When he realized what was calling out to him, he set out in search of it.

The gemstone dealers were eager to help, for he was an excellent client who purchased the best and rarest gems. He explained what he was looking for, and they began searching for it. He knew the odds of finding it were close to zero. He'd be more likely to be struck by lightning, for the rare stone he wanted was only found under black ice.

When he finished, he went home to wait in the house high on the black cliffs above Winters Lee. What he required was in motion now. It would lead where it would.

*

My name is Avalon, and I am still changing. I never know if it's going to be for better or worse, so it's time for me to write down my history. So Harry Houdini will understand how I ended up in Winters Lee. Here goes.

*

I married too young the first time after being ejected from the bitter, bereaved bosom of an impoverished family who had lost their inheritances of land, courage, and kindness. I was the runt of the family, small and skinny with wild, dark hair that stuck out all over. It had its own mind, just like I did.

My parents were worn out by life by the time I came along, so my oldest sister, a teenager who fancied going on the stage, chose Avalon Blue for my name. I became used to people's disbelief and laughter when they heard my odd, ridiculous name.

I formed no strong or lasting attachments to anyone in my family. They were loud, proud, hasty and quarrelsome. Our house was in a constant uproar. After enough conflicts with them, for it was in my nature to be impetuous, I learned to shut up and stay out of their way. I took up reading for companionship; like Robinson Crusoe, but female, I lived as though I was alone on an island.

The years sped by as I avoided family life and its conflicts and steadily built up a fantasy world in my mind. In time, I developed a melancholy tendency to compare my life to those of the heroines in the novels I read, causing me to be forever gloomy and disappointed. I was too young to know the stories were mostly glorified and unreal. Back then, I believed they were true, that life could be like it was in those books.

I lived in chaos and the disharmony of poverty and neglect and valued nothing except my books. I learned very little about my family. I didn't want to know who they were. Finally my family decided I was reading too much in reaction to my avoiding them. They took my books away, and banned them from the house. I saw no choice but to stay outside, so I spent as much time as the weather allowed in the fields and forest near home. I climbed trees in the woods and found one that fit my body and slept there when I was tired. I stayed out in the rain and hid behind the blue morning glories at the end of the garden.

The more I moved into the world of the outdoors, the more the silence inside me grew. I began to learn, to intuit, to discover the beautiful intelligence that can only be heard when the silence within us interacts with Nature. The depth and scope of it was, and remains beyond description. The realms of my soul began to expand past the written word. I started to feel a beautiful wisdom coming from Nature.

I learned to listen to the different moods of the wind, to foretell the patterns it would take. My hearing improved as my inner silence grew. I heard the corn in the fields squeak and groan as they outgrew the husk. I learned where the birds and squirrels nested and where they traveled to and from. I knew where the little red crawdads holed up in the creek running behind the cornfield.

After a while, I found my own way to be with people. I made little people and sofas and houses out of the smooth, gray clay lining the creek bank where the red crawdads lived and watched me. Once in a while, one of the crawdads got brave and tried to pinch me. At first, I ran away. Later, I danced out of their reach then teased them with twigs. I made up stories about the clay people. In all the stories, I was a grown up. I was strong and courageous and not afraid, and I lived in my own place.

Things went on that way until the day came when the mayhem and madness turned itself on me again. How could I not recognize the writing on the wall? It was time to leave.

In a few days, I packed what little belonged to me into a large paper sack and set out on the road. They watched me leave, but didn't try to stop me. I was scared and hurt and mad at them for not trying to stop me.

Before the day ended, I found a place to stay in town. An elderly couple agreed to give me room and board in exchange for working for them. Their home was cavernous, quiet and gloomy. I polished silver, cleaned carpets, did laundry, dishes, and anything else they needed done. They let me live in the attic and gave me simple food and a small allowance. Although I missed Nature, it felt good to be in a place where I could do my school homework, read books, and sleep in peace.

My family never came after me. They didn't want me, and it hurt. I guess they had their own troubles and were too busy with them to think of me.

But going backwards wasn't to be. I couldn't finish my old dreams. I had to dream forward. The people in town knew my large, unruly family, and knew I was one of them. They assumed I was cut from the same cloth, so they talked the old couple into getting rid of me. Before long, I found myself outside their front door, locked out of their house with my few belongings stuffed in a sack. There was no note, nothing to explain why.

I slept under bushes and in the town park until I found another place to stay. I went to school early and cleaned up in the bathroom each morning before classes. I managed to stay with four different families before I was forced to quit school and go to work full-time to support myself. Bitterly, I left behind the dreams I once cherished of getting a higher education.

Several years flew by. I became more silent, more shy. I worked hard, but there was very little money left after my living expenses were paid. The growing loneliness and desperation inside me grew stronger. They needed connection and to be seen. I tried to find people to make friends with, but between my family's bad reputation and my awkward silence and lack of social skills, I never found anyone.

I could not return to my beloved forests and hills and creeks of home again. They belonged to someone else now, a girl who wandered the woods and streams of long ago. The stories and strengths I built up over the years faded. I was no longer a secret heroine, neither my own, nor anyone else's. Now I was forced to live in town and work hard to survive. I bowed my head and bent my back to the hard task life had handed me.

I couldn't get the help I needed so I married an older man for security. In return, I waited on him hand and foot and took care of his mother while he traveled the country, selling insurance policies to businesses.

We had two children before he died of a heart attack one night in a small town in Kansas. The young woman traveling with him said she just met him that day and they were just friends. Sure. I took the children and most of the money we'd saved and left his cantankerous mother, who was quite surprisingly healthy, to fend for herself in the dark, gloomy house where we all lived.

We went on with our lives, but I felt more alone than ever, so I married a second time to a man who believed that work was the answer to everything. He ignored my children. We rarely saw him, for he was busy working. That marriage didn't last long. One day, tired of me not working as much and as hard as he thought I should, he angrily packed up and moved out without a backward glance. I was relieved he was gone. So were my children.

I had my own tiny house and a job to support us and I got by. Before long a sort of bedraggled, forlorn hope began squeaking through the door of my life again. The house needed repairs and my boring job was long and monotonous, but I was enjoying the freedom of not answering to anyone else.

Meanwhile, my ex-husband walked straight into my family's welcoming arms. Together, they loudly told anyone who would listen about my laziness and wrong doings. The lies spread fast through the circle of people I grew up with. I became cold and distant with them so I could handle yet another round of the familiar hurt.

In the first few years after he left, I felt flattened. I dressed in utility gray and took the blame for anything anyone put on me without protest. People said disrespectful and rude things to me and I was ignored as though I had no soul. And I let them.

Rarely did I feel the fleeting touches of the heroic, bold, laughing girl I once was. My little soul dancer was either broken or hidden away somewhere, and I didn't have her forwarding address. I didn't know where she lived now. My courage was gone, lost along with the daring spirit I read about in books when I was growing up. I couldn't find it anymore, and I lived in secret shame of that loss.

Then, one day, I realized I it was time to go forward again. My self-indulgent pity and grief must stop, or I would die a slow, sorrowful death while living out a self sacrificing life of misery.

That's when I began traveling. Where could I go? I possessed no car or money, so I started walking all over town. Then I bought a junk car and learned to drive. I felt like I'd passed through prison gates the first time I drove out of town in my own car. All three of us, me and the children, cussed mightily and happily that day.

Time passed. The children grew up and left, taking their suitcases and cars with them. They wanted to travel with someone else now. They were happy to get away. I accepted it and moved on, alone again.

I drove everywhere by myself. I camped by old mineral springs in desolate deserts. I searched through solemn churches and colorful art galleries. I sat on high, windy hills and traveled through dark nights on lonely roads with the moon and stars shining high above me.

Once I read about a people who walked their troubles away, so I tried it. It became true for me too. I walked the town, and rode and flew in my dreams and in my real life, and little by little, my childhood dreams returned.

Then one holy night, I discovered the girl I used to be was traveling with me again. She stayed with me and we traveled through cactus deserts with dark-eyed people and took part in ceremonies in the pouring rain. She laughed and ate squirrel stew around a campfire in a forest, taking the same nourishment from it her ancestors took. That girl rented a boat and rowed out on a sunny, isolated lake, took her clothes off and lay in it naked, sunbathing. She stood out in summer thunder storms with the wind blowing and the rain pouring down in warm sheets. She slept in her car, in tents and in teepees, motel rooms, and a few mansions. She stood on high hills in the wind and sometimes dressed like a wayward child just for the hell of it. She bought an apron and learned to cook Brussel sprouts with bacon instead of cabbage. She walked and walked, then walked some more. In the sun. In the rain. It didn't matter. She needed all of them if she was ever going to have a chance at becoming whole again. Each step mattered. Each step was a stitch taken to weave the parts and spaces of herself back together again.

Eventually, the girl I once was grew strong again and stood within me, unwavering. No more acceptance of being a doormat. No more being a second best anything. Life was good and could be fun, but it was time to go find out if the heroines in the books withstood or withdrew, like I once did. Maybe they came alive after reading about themselves. Maybe they blazed a path for people like me to walk. It was a clear message. All we needed to do now was find my path. It was time to go out on quest.

Plaid skirts have been made of lamb's wool since the weaving of cloth was invented. But Merino wool only comes from Merino sheep.

Chapter 16.   Aunt Amelia

I took up reading again. Only this time, I read the metaphysical and healing arts and sciences, searching for ways and words to define the nature of my life. Everything I read led right back to my family, so I began to research them. That's when I came across Great Aunt Amelia. She was an older relative who'd never met my parents or siblings. I guess they traveled in different circles, so to speak. She lived alone in a big house by the sea, somewhere in the south.

None of my family or relatives ever visited her. They said she was crazy and left her alone. They didn't like that she never married and lived a "normal" life, like they did. They said living alone made her too uppity to put up with, and she better never darken their doorstep asking for help.

I wrote to her and told her I was crazy too, from searching for who I was. We formed an immediate attachment. She asked me to call her Aunt Amelia, and through her letters, encouraged me to continue my search. I searched and still couldn't find a roost to settle on, so when she sent a letter inviting me to visit, I jumped at the chance and flew my little empty coop.

She took me under her wing and into her home. Aunt Amelia was tall, athletic and thin, with closely cropped white wavy hair, a long, patrician nose, and a great deal of dignity. She lived simply and almost sparsely. She was an avid gardener. We grew and picked our own vegetables. She kept a running conversation going with the green beans and the corn. She was proper, modest and smart, well-read and educated. She'd traveled the world.

She said she was in love once. She showed me his gravestone. It was in her family plot. On the stone was engraved, "Master Ronald B. Alderman, gone but never forgotten."

"Why is he buried here?"

"He was a distant cousin, and I wanted to keep him close. He died shortly before we were to be married."

"What did he die of?" I asked.

"It was a fight with another man." She spoke with a decisive note in her voice that told me there would be no more discussion on that sore subject.

Everything went smoothly, except for one small hitch that nagged at me frequently. Aunt Amelia owned a small sailboat, and she liked to take that damned boat out on sunny afternoons. I couldn't swim. I was terrified of water. I couldn't bring myself to get in the boat with her, so I watched her anxiously from shore. I sat somewhere and pretended to be reading, or tried to look like I was just casually strolling up and down the beach until she steered her little boat back in.

Such a long time ago! What a picture we must have made! Aunt Amelia clad in her old-fashioned bathing garb, competent and shouting songs or swearing at the ropes of the boat, and I, an old, fearful, barefoot child in my usual disarray of gray dress. How I hated that boat!

In the evenings, Aunt Amelia told me stories about the family we belonged to. Through her, I learned about my maternal great-grandmother's healing abilities. She laid hands on people and drove out their numbness and anything too cold within them. Healing frostbite was her specialty. Anything that needed heat to heal, she could heal it, but every time she lived in a house over three years it burned down, so she kept moving from house to house. She owned a fiery temper, was impatient, and married many times.

Her stories started me thinking. My parents, brothers, and sisters and I hadn't spoken since my ex-husband left me, when they helped him start trouble for me, but I still remembered the old days, the times between the troubles, when the best came out in them.

During those times, they displayed humor and grace. All of them were beautiful, and though I touched just the edges of their lives, I loved them.

Sometimes Aunt Amelia and I read to each other or played card games. She liked to gamble and enjoyed winning, but she didn't have much competition from me. She was a wise woman, content with life. I wondered how she got that way, so I asked her about the meaning of life.

She answered me concisely with humor and kindness. "What the hell are you searching for?" she asked me. "What in life could be so troubling as to cause you to run around like a lost waif who can't find her bread or a wand to wave in the air?"

I searched deep for an answer while she waited. I shrugged. I became like a dog worrying a bone.

"I don't know, damn it! It's very frustrating!"

She nodded. Her mouth thinned down.

"You better take hold of something soon. There's too many in our bunch that went south, and I don't mean literally."

After the house was locked up for the night, I went to my room and read all kinds of what was supposed to be helpful literature until I fell asleep.

Time flew by. A larger restlessness began to consume me. It made me impatient and ornery, even surly. Aunt Amelia heard the growing impatience in my voice, and though I didn't know it yet, she knew I'd reached a dead end.

I was drifting into depression and hopelessness. I was becoming a lost soul again. That girl needed something more. That girl kept throwing images of nature and animals and things at me in desperation, but I couldn't catch on to what she needed. I needed to figure it out soon, though, because without her, I was a loner again. I was also wasting time resenting the time and effort I had already expended on her behalf, believing that being lost had ended forever when we joined ranks again.

At times I caught Aunt Amelia looking at me speculatively. I shrugged it off. There was too much on my plate. I was becoming overwhelmed again, and I expected to lose her like I always lost everybody else.

One night after an especially fine dinner, I was laying back in my chair in my usual utility gray enjoying a pleasant food stupor, when Aunt Amelia announced that we were going shopping the next morning.

"What for?"

"We're going to buy you luggage and new clothes that aren't gray."

I sat up. "Where are we going?"

She frowned at me and said, "First of all, we are going to get you out of your prison garb. There is no prison around here. No more gray for you!"

"Where are we going?" I asked again. She sighed loudly. A look of determination came over her face.

I'm not going anywhere, you are!"

I stared at her, speechless with surprise.

"I attended a retreat on an island years ago, and it changed my life. I'm sending you there! They can help you."

I glared at her in shock.

"It's only for a short time!" she said, spreading out her hands pacifically. I didn't know what Aunt Amelia's age was, but she was incredibly old. The retreat she attended had to have been a long time ago.

I wasn't going to any such thing! Besides, what was the theme of the retreat? Rubbing bowls and chanting? Tramping through a jungle loaded with bugs? Eating brown rice and drinking stale water on some godforsaken island with no sunscreen? My skin was too old for that stuff!

I fired questions at her. She answered some of them, but she was purposefully vague on others. She explained that the retreat was on a stunningly beautiful island owned by a group of pleasant, gentle, peaceful Shaman women who worked in various healing arts. Yes, other nice women went there all the time, but she was not allowed to tell me where this lovely, mysterious island resort was located, because it was extremely private and exclusive.

"There is nothing to be afraid of!" she said, trying to stop the conversation. "Consider it an adventure, if nothing else!"

"I am not going!" I protested.

"You will go," she stated coldly. "I don't expect any more of you than I have ever expected of myself. I already did it, and here I am, alive and better off for it!"

I resorted to whining, "I don't want to give up eating what I like or reading. I like being alone."

She responded tartly, "You left those things behind before and survived them very well!" She jumped to her feet and said, "It's time for you to move on, to go forward. I won't listen to a lifetime of whining from you, or put up with your self-induced depression, or watch you indulge yourself in ridiculous misery, so you can either go to the retreat or leave this house! It is entirely up to you!"

She marched out of the room. I shook my head in shock. She took the wind right out of my sails! Maybe she was right. Maybe I needed massage and tropical music to soothe my wounded soul, or whatever it was that kept me spending my whole life chasing something I couldn't define in words.

An image of drinks with little umbrellas in them, smiling women speaking in low, gentle voices, salad dinners to thin me down, and cool sheets to slide under in an air conditioned room after dancing the night away on a terrace surrounded by hibiscus flowers, flowed gently into my mind. I guess I could be brave. Besides, I'd been through tougher adventures. This one should be a breeze! I grew meek, and was ready to go shopping the next morning.

*

I left for the mysterious island resort with three pieces of luggage and a ton of things packed in boxes, gifts Auntie was sending to the women on the island. She said she would be waiting for me when I was done. I asked her how long I would have to stay. She shrugged and said, "I don't know. Why, does it matter?"

She looked up and away at a cloud and smiled at it. "Just enjoy yourself."

Puzzled, I watched her. She was doing it again. Addressing her words to the white clouds high above us in the blue sky. I frowned at her. Lately, she'd developed a disconcerting habit of speaking to the ground, a tree, or a wall whenever we talked about the island. I hoped her odd new habit would soon pass and wasn't a sign of aging.

A well-placed decorative pin can liven up the most embarrassing of gabardine outfits.

Chapter 17.   The Island

Three women met me at the island's boat dock. They were very formal with a stately air about them. They wore colorful, flowing caftans, their hair dressed in elaborate crowns on top of their heads. One of them greeted me without a smile. The other two never spoke.

I trailed along behind them as they walked down a thin dirt path leading between palm trees to a dirt track wide enough for a cart to travel. The woman that greeted me spoke again.

"There are no cars allowed on this island."

We climbed into a horse drawn cart. What I could see of the island on the ride to the resort was beautiful. There were garden spots with neat rows of plants in them and fruit and banana trees mixed in with splashes of colorful flowers and other shrubs.

Very nice! We stopped before a cluster of small, rustic wood cabins. The women grabbed my luggage and escorted me to a cabin. I stepped in and surveyed my surroundings. The cabin was one large room. A simple rope hammock with a colorful quilt on it hung in a corner. Sheer white curtains covered window openings to soften the tropical sunlight and let in cool air. A small wood table, two chairs and a sink with a short shelf above it served as the kitchen. A tiny earthen oven was built into one wall. A simple wood dresser stood against a wall with wood pegs above it for hanging clothes.

The walls were painted white and the hard-packed dirt floor was clean. Cold spring water ran over rocks, tinging into a metal basin in a corner. The water sang a muted song while it cooled the air inside the cabin. I clapped my hands in appreciation.

"What a clever way to disguise a resort and to fit in with nature!"

I looked around for the hidden phone, bathroom, and menus, but didn't see any. The women stared at me with impassive faces.

"This is not a resort. It is a Shamanic training school," one of the women stated flatly.

"The outhouse is back there."

She flung an arm towards the back of the cabin.

"Come to the central house for dinner," she said, pointing to the left to indicate the location. They turned on their heels and walked out. I stood there as the realization of what had just happened clicked in my mind. Shamanic! No wonder Aunt Amelia had stared at anything but me when she talked about this island! I chased after the women.

"I've changed my mind! I want to go home!' I wailed loudly at their retreating backs. They turned around and watched me skid to a stop in front of them.

"There is no going back until you are finished. Remember what you came here for."

I searched their faces hopefully, but found no pity. My mind raced frantically through my options. There was no phone, and they meant exactly what they said. I was trapped, caught like a rat on a remote island with what looked, so far, like a bunch of overdressed, nutty zealots. No way out. I bowed to the inevitable, heaved a deep sigh, and turned back to unpack my luggage and settle in. What else could I do? I would figure a way out somehow. Later.

The next morning, I began learning the routines I would follow while residing on the island, at least until I could figure out how to run away. But there was never any time to think about it, and well, maybe I would learn something that would bind me to myself again. So I stayed, half-hearted about the whole running away thing, one day mad as blazes at Aunt Amelia, the next day grateful for the opportunity.

A different Shaman woman came to get me each morning while it was still dark. There were no clocks anywhere, so who the hell knew what time it was? It was way too early, in my opinion. I needed coffee. None of them told me their names, though I introduced myself. Very politely, I might add.

We hiked to different spots on the island while each of them explained the vegetation, the trees, the soil, whatever, to me while I daydreamed of coffee, featherbeds and steaks. The walks were long. It took me a few days to learn to wake up before dawn, then to keep up with the pace they set. After a while, I realized they were working to increase my physical health and stamina. I finally got to eat a small, simple healthful breakfast of eggs, fruit, nuts, and bread with no smiles or added condiments when the daily hike was over.

Communal meals were held in the long, low central house. The women running the island conducted a variety of activities in the shade under the open sided, airy building. I took classes with a small group of women in the afternoon. None of us were allowed to speak to each other. I learned that the women teaching us were different kinds of Shamans, the designated healers of their people. They differed from each other in appearance and age, but they seemed to have no problem working together.

I felt the power radiating from them, collectively and individually. They were strong and intimidating, ornery and abrupt with a weird sense of humor. They laughed at me more than the others who, no doubt, knew what they were getting into before they landed here on Hell's Island.

Some of the Shaman women lived on the island year round. Others came for training we weren't allowed to ask about.

Everything they did seemed to have a purpose. I didn't know what they were going to put me through. I didn't know if I could do it, and the impending sense of doom kept me blabby and nervous. Not to mention that my hair had gone white because I didn't have access to hair color. They laughed and volunteered to color it blue for me when I asked where I get could hair color. I turned and ran and didn't ask again.

I knew without a doubt that I was in over my head. I thought briefly of bribes as an option, but the women never gave me much time to think about anything. There was no choice except to carry on with the daily chores assigned to me, shut up, and wait. I weeded in the large vegetable gardens and worked in the vast kitchen. They gave me lessons in how to paint, how to use my voice and hands properly in rituals, and what different rituals required.

I became accomplished at several small rituals and felt vain about them. I imagined myself returning to the world, an accomplished

Shaman standing tall and lithe, (as much as I could) dressed in a slimming toga of some sort of lightweight material floating around me in becoming colors while I performed rituals. In my imagination, I was surrounded by awed, admiring faces and huge crowds while I did the rituals. People were healed left and right, and happily provided me with all the acclaim and food and shelter I would ever need. And hair color products. I pictured myself in my dotage, being cared for and revered as a holy woman.

Of course, I never told anyone else what I was thinking. I was starting to suspect that this retreat *had* been a good idea! I began to think fondly of Aunt Amelia again instead of cursing the day she was born. She was a wise woman, indeed!

Introducing lace into an already planned design can be incredibly exciting-or maximumly treacherous!

Chapter 18.   The Black Horse

Early one morning before daybreak, without any warning, a group of Shaman women showed up at my door. I took a deep breath. I was in trouble. "Uh oh!" I muttered. Where one or more of these women were gathered, there was always big trouble. I was instantly terrified.

They wore solemn looks. They were dressed in the formal clothes and animal skins worn for performing rituals. Some of them wore highly decorated and colorful clothes. Others were carefully plain. All of them wore small leather pouches around their necks. Others had larger pouches hanging from the leather belts around their waists.

All the Shaman women worked with "totem" in the rituals they did. They explained to us in class that a "totem" was a symbol representing an animal or a plant's spirit qualities and abilities. Each animal or plant represented a "seat" of the ancient clan each of us humans belongs to—a "seat" being an ancient, first basic building block in our genetic lineage. Each of those animals or plants were our "totem" and worked with different parts of the cumulative self; both the mundane and sacred aspects of it.

I stepped back, took a deep breath, then nodded to them. There was no choice. I would have to trust these powerful women. My plans to run away never bore any fruit; they crumbled into ashes. My hopeful visualizations of racing away from them on a fast horse, yelling, "Ha-ha!" back at them and jumping into a fast boat that raced farther and farther away from the island, fell apart while they waited for me to dress.

"I have some Day Glo Hormone Cream in my suitcase. If you would like to stay here, I could give you facials," I offered hopefully. No go.

We left the cabin in the dark. I grudgingly trudged after them. I needed coffee. Didn't anyone on Hell's Island own a thermos? We walked in silence for a long time. I began to recognize some of the landmarks. We were headed for the western end of the island. At last we reached the bottom of a steep hill close to the outer tip of the island. I could hear the roar of surf to the side of us, though I couldn't see it.

The women climbed a smooth, thin dirt path winding up the side of a steep hill. I wondered how many feet had traveled this path and where it led to. I followed them up the steep trail as best as I could. At the top of the hill was a cave, partially hidden by smooth branched trees with red twisted trunks and broad green leaves. I followed them into the cave. It was dim and cool inside. After my eyes adjusted to the cave's dimness, I looked around. It was big. I shuddered to think of what it once sheltered.

The hard, ochre yellow and red dirt floor was smooth and clean. Bowls, candles and other things were stacked against the red clay walls.

The women placed lit candles around the cave. In the center of the red dirt floor was a deep, round fire pit filled with wood. We sat down in a circle around it. One of the women lit the fire. It flamed up hot and strong.

The fire keeper began chanting and throwing herbs on the flames. The herbs exuded a strange scent. Someone covered the entrance to the cave. We sat in the dark watching the fire. The flames in the fire pit threw black, elongated, dancing reflections onto the red clay walls. The cave grew hotter and hotter.

Some of the Shaman women started drumming. I grew more apprehensive. They drummed for what seemed like forever in the strangely scented air. The drumming grew faster. My heart started pounding. I began intuiting an intent and purpose forming behind their drumming. What were they going to do to me?

I was scared to death, and resented their not telling me more about the ritual they intended for me but they didn't care. They just kept on drumming and chanting. A long time passed. I grew tired of worrying. Exhausted, I slumped forward, my head down. The women instantly laid down squares of cloth and poured powder from their pouches into them, as though my slumping forward was a signal.

I didn't care. I just wanted to sleep. They passed a bucket and dipper around the circle and urged me to drink. The water tasted like green lilies. Everyone else took a drink, poured a bit of water on their powders and passed the bucket on before they mixed the powders into colorful pastes with their fingers.

Two of the Shaman women knelt behind me and whispered in my ears. I didn't understand their words. More women knelt on each side of me. They painted my face, then pulled me to my feet and ordered me to take off my clothes. When I was naked, one of them announced they were going to tattoo the lines of the first of the sacred animals assigned to me on my body.

I didn't give a damn. I suspected I was in an altered state, lounging on the Main Street of the town of Serendipity from the fabulous herbs in the water or the fire or both. They could've tattooed me to the wall and I wouldn't have cared. This sneaky bunch had led me into an altered space without my permission. But so what? I felt good. There was no going back anyway. So why not go forward happy and stoned?

They began a strange chant. I closed my eyes and leaned on them. They lowered me to the floor. I dozed in and out of a happy stupor while they tattooed animal lines on me. I admit, the process bordered on being sharp and painful sometimes, and it seemed to take forever. I passed the time by dreaming of being a tattoo artist with skills much superior to theirs. I dreamed of pearl handled tattoo guns with matching leather holsters, my name tooled on them, and me naked with large, perky breasts, whipping out my tattoo guns and aiming them at strategic locations on anyone I didn't like. Guess who that happened to be at that moment? Aunt Amelia.

My happy trance state ended abruptly when I felt the lines begin to move. Startled, I opened my eyes and scrambled to my feet. Something weird was happening, and I definitely didn't like it! The lines felt like strings attached to me. Tattoos weren't supposed to move, were they? I felt the lines tighten. I couldn't get free of them. Nervously, I looked around and saw the women holding thin, shimmering lines of Light in their hands. The lines were attached to me.

I screamed, but it came out sounding like a horse's whinny. That was odd. The women jumped back. One of them stood up and shouted something in a commanding voice that echoed through the cave. Someone shoved a dipper of water to my mouth and urged me to drink. I drank thirstily. I felt like I hadn't had a drink in years! I couldn't get enough. The water left a sweet taste in my mouth, like new mown hay. The taste and smell of it brought an image to me. I fell to the floor and began to dream again.

Once upon a time, long ago, I was a shiny black horse cropping sweet grass down by the beach on this island, and I had run across the fields and into the cave where the women captured me. I felt them pull some kind of strings tighter on the horse I was in my dream. I wanted to run from the cave. I cried out and fought the ropes that kept me from my freedom. My fear grew. I began to dance and buck, desperately trying to throw off the ever tightening ropes that held me. A second drum beat began. The horse thought the drumming was the sound of hooves. It tried to run away and join the other horses.

The ropes tightened again. The black horse did not want to be in this dark, hot cave. It wanted to be free to roam the island, to crop grass and stand in the sun without a care. It wanted to stretch its legs and run fast as the wind past anything that ever needed carrying.

The black horse shivered and strained and fought against the ropes for a long time. At last it broke into a sweat, lowered its head and stood still. It was thirsty again. The women held the dipper to the horse's mouth and it drank and drank. Then it sank to the earth, fell over on its side, and slept.

In its dreams, the horse roamed the Earth freely, only answering to its own kind and Spirit. The Shaman women ran their hands over the horse, chanting as the living lines of the black horse settled into place on the skin of the sleeping woman.

I woke up in the cave and lay there, watching the firelight flickering off the walls. I was laying on the cool dirt floor, wrapped in a soft blanket. I felt peaceful and serene. Something had ended. I didn't care what it was. I sat up. Someone handed me a dipper of water. I drank. I felt my right hip throbbing. I ran my hand over it and felt some kind of ointment. One of the women grabbed my hand away from it. She shook her head no at me and urged me to lay back down. I did, and instantly fell into a dreamless sleep.

I woke up later and left the cave to pee. One of the women went with me. We went back inside the cave, and I put my clothes on. The women seemed pleased with what happened.

They ignored my questions. We left the cave and went back down the hill. They led me to a bathing stream. I splashed into it and stayed there a long time. I felt like I couldn't get enough water. The Shaman women poured water over me, then soused me up and down until I was waterlogged, and all the paints were gone from my body. Then they wrapped me in a robe and walked me back to my cabin. They waited until I dressed in clean clothes and ate sparingly from the bowls of food on the table. Then they led me to the bed, and I fell asleep again.

Early the next morning, the door to the cabin flew open. Chattering, laughing women noisily made their way into the room. They were happy and exuded vitality. I sat up and glared at them. I had something like a giant hangover, plus the beginnings of a queen-sized pity party. I was in no mood for their cheerfulness. Besides, it was barely daylight outside. Again. Weren't they just the early birds!

The women held brushes, bottles, and jars of paint. They laughed at my expression. They carried in paint buckets, large pieces of canvas and more brushes and tossed them happily into a big pile in the middle of the floor. What the hell did they expect from me now? Surely, they didn't expect me to paint this place or something like that! After what I went through,

I needed to lay around and gently mull over my experience. I needed to bring my equine experience into some sort of soothing spiritual construct I could understand and begin to feel good about. That hadn't happened yet.

I might even need to "ohm" a little. That's what happened at "normal" retreats; it was what was expected! Didn't they know anything here? I needed to be gently led into a new spiritual understanding of what I experienced with silence, tasteful foods, and beautiful words.

They shouted at me. They ordered me to get up off my ass. They said it was time for me to paint the horse. I was to nail a canvas drop cloth to the wall to paint on. I was to lay the other drop cloths down carefully so the paint wouldn't get on the floor. Then they all started happily yelling at me to get my lazy ass up and get started. I was to tell them when the painting was done. I could take all the time I needed, but I was to begin it right now. They left in a bunch, noisily slamming the door behind them.

I waited in the silence. Was this another trick or a joke?

"I won't do it!" I muttered to myself. I lay down, punched my pillow and indignantly turned my face to the wall. In every other spiritual experience, I was given time to assimilate and contemplate the results before I was told to do something else. Sometimes it took weeks. I was respected. I assumed it was that way everywhere, and with everyone. Big mistake!

Bitterly I opened one eye and stared at the pile of stuff in the middle of the cabin floor. Besides, I hadn't taken enough paint lessons yet. I never in my life painted anything before the painting lessons I endured here. I didn't have the faintest clue how to draw or paint people or things. And now I was supposed to paint a horse I'd never seen? Good luck!

I lay on the bed, trying to stay mellow, listening to the quiet surrounding me. I was going to have it my way. I wouldn't do what they ordered. I hummed a little and listened to the spring water tinging pleasantly into the metal basin. Then I started wondering why they wanted me to do this. They always knew more than I did, I thought bitterly. I speculated awhile on that but came up with nothing. It was true. They did know more than me. And it was going stay that way. Oh well.

After a while, the bed turned into a rock. I imagined my right hip hurt worse than it did. After all, I was no spring chicken! I thought about the Shaman women mixing the shiny black color of the horse and painting me with it. Finally I admitted to myself that I was filled with energy. The water and rest and food refreshed me, so I got off my lazy ass and got started.

First I sorted the buckets, then I drew clean water and laid the brushes out in order on the kitchen table. That made sense. I nailed a drop cloth to the wall left of the front door and spread drop cloths below it. I drew the horse on the drop cloth. It didn't look like a horse, but who cared? I sorted through the paints to find the right mix for the deep, shiny black of the horse and later, for the red clay walls inside the cave.

That night, laying in my bed, I ran my hand over my hip. The thin, glowing horse lines ran steadily across it. I kept my hand on them and fell asleep.

Each day I arose at sunrise. No laying around or sleeping in this island paradise! I swept the hearth around the big cooking fire after meals, carried scraps to the compost pile, peeled, chopped and cooked vegetables and attended classes.

I worked on the painting in my spare time. I painted the round, red clay cave walls behind the horse. Then I added a fire and drums, the Shaman women, and electric blue lines everywhere. As a special touch, I added the weird red tree outside the cave and a few lightning bolts striking the Shaman women's sorry asses. I thought about it, and painted over the lightning bolts. Better safe than sorry.

One day the painting was finished. The black horse danced in the middle of the red cave with the red twisted tree and shale boulders outside the cave. Huge women in shamanic garb oversaw the horse's dance. They held pots of paint in their hands. A slice of innocent blue sky hung high above the cave, darkening down into midnight blue, surrounding the cave as it worked its way down to the bottom of the canvas. Someone else might looked at it and see blobs but I saw my ritual in it.

I cleaned the brushes and paint pots and put everything in order. The women came and looked at the finished painting. The next day when I returned to the cabin, the painting was gone. The women had taken it away. I was surprised that I missed it so much. I went to the lodge and asked for it back, but they said no, they had another use for it. But I did a good job, they told me. And they knew who the lightning bolts were intended for. At that point, I thought I best leave. I got up hastily and ran out the door, their laughter following me.

Sometimes a mentor gets woven into the lining of our lives. That is, if we are lucky.

Chapter 19.   The Venerable Hare

A few days later, the Shaman women came for me again. We made the long trek to the cave on the west end of the island.

"This is getting to be a habit!" I muttered to them. They didn't answer, so I complained, trying to be funny, "This is a hell of a way to get a painting done!"

They acted like they didn't hear me. What was new from this large, unpredictable, but well dressed, towering bunch of tight lipped, bad ass Amazons?

We hiked through a rugged landscape softened by rosy morning light. A golden dawn of mauve, orange and red was just topping the steep hill at the end of the island when we reached the cave. We stopped and watched the sun rise and grow brighter until it opened into its full majestic splendor, spreading across the sky in pinks, whites and oranges, layering gorgeous, necessary light onto the Earth.

We went inside the dark cave. The women covered the door opening. I looked up, for there had to be a place for the smoke to leave the cave. Above me were natural layered vents that drew the smoke up through the top of the cave and out into the outside air.

The Shaman women sat in the same places again. By now I knew some of their names. I looked into their faces and repeated their names to myself.

They started the fire and began humming and shaking rattles. They passed the water bucket. I was thirsty and drank all the water the dipper held. While I was drinking, a woman screamed, causing me to drop the dipper. She kept on screaming. Then she started thumping the floor of the cave. I stared at her, puzzled, ready to run. *What the hell was she doing?*

The other women started screaming. Their screams of fear filled my ears. My heart pounded with terror. I cowered and covered my ears. *Why are they so scared? Surely these extraordinary, larger than life, definitely left of center, badass, fearless Shaman women, who seemed to be familiar with every unseen spirit in existence and its purpose, good or bad, who held unquestioned authority over me, surely they could handle anything that came along!*

I hoped they didn't expect me to handle anything weird for them! I cringed and waited for the awful thing, whatever it was, to happen. Maybe a ghost would appear, or a demon. Who the hell knew?

My mind swiftly packed its suitcase and took flight. I became mindless and numb, frozen, not a new condition for me in these kinds of situations. *Onions,* I thought desperately, *I didn't cut up enough onions for the soup yesterday.*

My mind checked back in. I knew it was back for only a peek. The ominous thumping and screaming took on a familiar rhythm, one I recognized. I peered through the darkness, trying to scrutinize the Shaman women's faces. My mind couldn't make any sense of what was happening. Enough! I couldn't stand this and I wouldn't! Swift anger raced through me. I jumped to my feet, ready to run out of the cave.

The thumping and screaming stopped instantly. I stood weaving in mid-air in the sudden silence, completely confused. Stay or go. I couldn't make up my mind which one to do. I swayed back and forth in an agony of confusion while my mind frantically sought the better of the two choices.

The women watched and waited, silent and unhelpful, while I hovered on the brink. The fire seemed to grow bigger and hotter. I was sweating a river and soaking wet. I could hear my sweat pattering down on the cave floor. Bit by bit I calmed down. I started to sit back down. As soon as I did, the thumping and screaming started again. I shot back up, startled, terrified, and now, pissed off. *They were doing this to me on purpose! Why?*

I waited for them to stop, but they kept on screaming, staring at me with both contempt and compassion on their faces. I shuddered at the looks on their faces. What they felt for me looked horrifyingly familiar. Their looks of contempt took me back to ugly times, to mean people, to bitter places. Something big and awful I had avoided forever rose to the surface. I groaned and belched out humiliation and pure, unadulterated shame. It was old and gross and stunk like rotten eggs.

I never wanted anyone to know how ridiculously easy it was for anyone to take me over, make me mind and take my precious life and time from me, with me pretending I was doing what they wanted out of choice. I wasn't brave, I was a coward. In a blinding instant, I accepted my cowardice.

I whirled and bolted out of the cave. I heard the Shaman women chasing me. They were screaming the names of every kind of cowardice at me. I raced away from their hurtful words, feathering the edges of brush, stumbling over rocks. I'd wanted to run like this all my life. Countless faces and voices streamed behind me, chasing me madly, screaming names and insults at me. Past loves, children, family, anyone, everyone, chased after me, screaming, trying to trap me. But I outran them all.

I ran until I was past exhaustion before I stopped and turned to face them. A sense of exhilaration and power filled me. I didn't care anymore. It was over. Out in the open.

But only the Shaman women stood before me, soaked, sweating and panting. All the others who had chased after me forever were gone. So were their words.

I cocked my head and listened to the fresh new silence. It was the first time there was silence in that place since I was a blameless, innocent child, before I was told in anger how much I always hurt people, and what a coward I was. I sniffed the silence. It didn't stink any more. Tears streamed down my face.

The women surrounded me. I fell back into their arms. They held me in a living cradle made of their hands. I stared up at their faces in awe. There were all kinds of luminescent colors, thin lines of light running across their faces. They were beautiful!

They laid me down on the ground. I closed my eyes. I was so tired. I felt the sharp prick of something like a needle, but I didn't care. I opened my eyes again and stared up at the wisdom in their faces. I basked in the shine of their fierce, uncompromising, wise eyes as the lines of the Hare moved into place on my body. Tick tock. I had a new clock.

When it was over, the women walked me back to the cave. They pushed me down into a sitting position in front of the fire. Then they sat down and passed the water bucket around. The water tasted cool and sweet. Then they instructed me about the Rabbit and the Venerable Hare.

*

"Rabbits are vegetarians, not carnivores. They do not have the heart of a predator, so other animals assume they have no courage," one Shaman woman said.

Another said, "Rabbit is here to learn that it has another part of itself living high in the Heavens, a part instructing its Spirit. The spirit part of the Rabbit self is the Venerable Hare. Rabbit stops the world from cracking open when it becomes the Venerable Hare!"

I listened, puzzled.

"You put a Rabbit on me? All that hell, just to put a rabbit on me?"

They ignored my words.

"Rabbit does not like to leave its home. It wants to stay just a small Rabbit, but its destiny is to become the Venerable Hare. Everything that exists must strive towards its spiritual potential.

If Rabbit reaches high enough and becomes the Venerable Hare, it is forever committed to journeying to the end of the world at dusk and dawn each day to weave the beginning and end

165

of the world together so Time as we know it can exist, so the world doesn't crack open."

Another said, "The Venerable Hare is the Time Keeper standing between the two poles of Light and Dark, the polarity constantly creating our reality/world. It is a magic, active, terrible place.

The Time Keeper can never forget the Beginning and the End of the world, or it would not exist anymore. All is midnight and all is high noon, all at the same time. But Rabbit is always scared. It has many enemies, and no defenses."

"You put a Rabbit on me?" I asked again, still trying to understand.

"Rabbit is constantly stalked by Fear in the form of predators who know all about its Fear. Many times, its prey doesn't even have to kill it! It dies from being too scared.

"Only Rabbit owns the spiritual courage to weave this world together each time at the exact moment it is needed. No other totem can aspire to this. Only Rabbit, after it becomes the Venerable Hare."

"Courage is not under the dominion of any one species," another said. "That is why Rabbit has become your Teacher. Your culture tells you what to fear and instills shame in you for entertaining those fears, all at the same time.

"All of Life has courage in it. Courage comes in many different forms. When you stop running, you have the potential to become the Venerable Hare! Those were the two sides of life you felt when you couldn't make up your mind whether to stay or run."

Another Shaman woman added, "Many indigenous cultures handle their spiritual learning by assigning animals, or totem, to their people in crisis. The animals represent the ancient, sacred Nature in which everyone shares."

"In our culture, we would see you as going through a never-ending spiritual crisis. That is why you are being assigned animal totem as Spirit teachers to learn from so you can end your crisis.

While the Venerable Hare is weaving the world back together, it observes the flood of life passing by and learns how Time works. As it learns, the Venerable Hare enters a new state of consciousness.

Everything makes the journey to that new place at some time in its life, so you must not run from the terror of life teaching you. Now is the time to unlearn the bad habit of thinking you are the boss of life. It is time for you to accept that there is something bigger going on. You are just a small part of it. You do not run the show."

"You put two Rabbits on me?" I asked stupidly.

The women dropped their solemn attitudes, shook their heads, and shouted with laughter.

"We should have put drunken Rabbit on you!"

By this time, I was dazed by all the new concepts they were trying to teach me. I felt overfull and stupid. I looked around at them, blinked, and closed my eyes. The voices went away, and I slept. Later, they walked me down the hill. The day grew heavy and dark. Rain fell, but nobody hurried as we paced the path back to my cabin.

*

I stopped trying to figure out how to run away. The little cabin became my sanctuary. The women and the chores became familiar to me. I gave up worrying about shaving my legs, growing excess armpit hair and wearing deodorant, for I was doused in water quite often, sometimes under protest. I went through more rituals in the red clay cave, shaded by the leafy, twisted, red tree on top of the hill at the west end of the island.

Each time we went to the cave, the Shaman women taught me the story of the animal and its spirit nature and why I needed it before or after they tattooed its lines on my body. Afterwards, they doused me in water and escorted me back to my cabin and instructed me to paint the animal on a canvas. I painted sixteen animals during the time I spent on the island.

I went to them once to complain that sixteen was an awful lot of animals. One a month would have been appropriate, I argued, but shut up as soon as the Shaman women said the usual number each one of them aspired to was sixty-seven. They laughed at the look of terror on my face as I fled.

I painted each animal, then the women came and took the painting away. While I painted, a thousand different thoughts ran through my mind.

At times I thought what I was doing was good and purposeful. Other times I thought it was the most insane thing anyone could ever have happen to them. Here I was, trapped on a secret island with no phones or menus, being taken into a dark, hot cave every so often by a bunch of no doubt deranged, certainly very left of center, hardheaded, intrepid, rugged, tough, bad ass Shaman women who were tattooing my body with living animal images during what should have been a soothing sauna. I used to be fond of saunas. Never again. I suggested opening a tattoo parlor to them as a joke; when they asked if I wanted to be the first client, I shut up and ran again.

God only knew the Shaman women's ages. I was accepting all this as though it was no problem. I was becoming a contented, tattooed woman, an illustrated woman. All I needed to complete my journey into my new world of aged, illustrated wisdom was a bottle of cheap wine, a motorcycle, and an old, testosterone-loaded bike rider who cussed a lot and spat sporadically.

If my children or anyone else found out that the cowardly little woman they knew was in the process of becoming a highly illustrated woman, they would have kidnapped me for my own protection, locked me up and thrown away the key.

Then again, what the hell did I have to lose? I was a "mature" older woman with a life that would no doubt, degenerate with further age into wrinkled obscurity. Marginalized old age offered endless gruesome possibilities, like getting fatter, balding, growing hair in weird places, using a walker, and becoming senile. Old age was mainly being lonely and ignored by family, left out of the mainstream and bored to death. And I never wanted to have a meaningful, loud conversation with my dead "Uncle Joe."

Those were only a few of the crummy choices available to older people. That, and aloneness inevitably ending in death. Grim. Not a fun picture. So how much worse could a little excitement be for an older person?

Boredom might kill a person quicker than an adventure!

Each day there was a vast, innumerable smorgasbord of thoughts to choose from. My mind was back, and it swiftly unpacked three or four Louis Vuitton suitcases, a couple duffle bags, and settled in.

So what if I was stuck on a tropical island I couldn't leave, one that didn't allow television or cars, had no fashion shops, and most important, without proper recourse to skin care. Yet here I was with a bunch of women who thought nothing of being rumored to be at least two hundred years old. I bet they wouldn't dream of using wrinkle cream!

And what about those guys who sit in one position and pray for forty years to reach "enlightenment?" How would a parent like having a son, since males are the only ones allowed; thank you, patriarchal B.S., pull a stunt like that? Never having any grandkids, nothing! A strict diet and not much conversation there, either!

There were languages spoken on this earth that I could never learn in a million years, all with different concepts undergirding them. People were killed on whims, brain-washed or taken as slaves. People disappeared; people lived in odd places; people yodeled on mountain tops; they fought their way through jungles searching for any number of strange things. People were creeps and angels and kids and grownups in costumes.

The world was, indeed and truly a stage, so I guess what I was doing didn't look so bizarre in the larger scheme of Life. A life not examined is not a well-lived life. Ha Ha. I think that's a quote from somebody.

Brocade is woven on shuttles, often made with or without silver and golden threads. It's anyone's guess as to which it will be.

Chapter 20. Tossed Out Into the World

Time passed quickly on the island. I was kept too busy to think about the outside world. I slipped into a nice routine that seemed likely to last forever. I didn't mind any more.

Then one day, a bunch of the Shaman women walked in the door of my cabin carrying large buckets of white paint. I wondered what they wanted me to paint now. Maybe they wanted me to whitewash myself? Or them? I grinned at the idea.

They set the paint down in the middle of the floor and ordered me to paint the cabin walls white. I didn't have a problem with that. I didn't ask why. I'd been down that futile road before.

One of them announced loudly, "When you are finished, you will leave the island."

My snug little world instantly fell apart at her astounding revelation. I was shocked into speechless fury. I had been here for months, and I assumed that these women were supposed to finish teaching me... AND remove the tattoos!

I had taken for granted that my transformation would be completed while I was on the island, the lines of the animals removed before I left.

"I can't go out in the world looking like this!" I shouted in consternation. "What the hell! You can't do this to me! What about the lines on me? You've marked me like a leper! I can't go back out in the world with these lines on me!"

I ran my hands over the thin glowing lines that moved whenever I was agitated. They were certainly moving now!

With finality, the women said, "You'll figure it out!" I followed them out the door, complaining desperately, but they ignored me.

"You've betrayed me!" I screamed at their retreating backs. I ran back and forth in front of the cabin, stomping and shouting. They kept going. I watched until they were out of sight. I fussed and carried on; at last I was forced to accept leaving. I would have to figure out how go back out into the world without their help.

Bitterly, I set about whitewashing the walls. I took my time, making the process last as long as possible, but that didn't bother the Shaman women at all. Nothing bothered them!

The time to leave drew near. I abandoned my anger. I went into stark fear, fell to my knees in front of them, and begged them to let me stay.

"Such drama!" they said admiringly, applauding loudly and vigorously. Then one of them spoke sternly, offering me the only advice I was to get from them. "You are a funny little clown! Like Sholley Chapelin!

I interrupted, "You mean Charlie, don't you?"

"No, we mean you can become a Sholley Chapelin. The only chance you have to become who you were meant to be is to go back out into the world you are so afraid of and face yourself there! Without the teachers you now carry, you couldn't do it. They will help you understand you."

*

I left the island wearing a long-sleeved, high-necked gray shirt and slacks in ninety degree weather. Furtively, like a criminal, I boarded the boat, and then a private plane back to Aunt Amelia's house.

"Is she ever going to get a piece of my mind!" I muttered furiously. She tricked me into undergoing this ordeal! It was all her fault that I was now covered with weird tattoos needing to be babied or they would act up so I had to pet them constantly to keep them in hiding.

They were picky about perfumes and a bunch of other things, too. I had to start using unscented soap or they acted up. I was eating organic. No more cookie binges. *They are highly allergic lines,* I realized bitterly. *Lines who sneezed and coughed and crawled out of hiding in protest each time I rebelled.*

Also, I was going to rat on the Shaman women. They weren't as nice as she said. They refused to engage in lengthy, meaningful conversations with me, they never let me make new friends, and there were no throw pillows or nail polish in the cabin. Furthermore, they had tattooed me all over, called me a funny little clown, laughed at me, and kicked my ass out!

*

I didn't question for one second that Aunt Amelia would find a way to help me fix my tattoo problem, but she just laughed at me, and said she couldn't. I was furious with her for sending me to the retreat, but she stayed calm in the face of my anger.

"You're taking yourself too seriously. There are many people in different cultures who tattoo themselves all over, and they wear them with pride."

"Oh yeah? How many of them have tattoos that move?"

She looked down her nose at me.

"I will admit THAT is a problem. But the lines ARE very thin....right? Why don't you quit complaining and do something useful to help yourself? What is, is!"

Then she tapped her long chin thoughtfully before she beamed at me.

"You could begin by researching the cultures around the world who tattoo themselves! Find out why they do it! You might learn something."

I retorted, "I bet theirs don't move!"

She retorted. "You don't know that!"

Several weeks passed. I hid out in my room and sulked. Aunt Amelia ignored me. One morning I couldn't stand it any longer. I was bored to death with cooping myself up. I went downstairs to the patio at the side of the rose garden where Aunt Amelia was trimming roses. She stopped and looked at me. I glared at her while she looked me up and down. I was wearing sunglasses, a baseball cap, gray slacks and a long-sleeved shirt. She leaned towards me and spoke in a confidential tone.

"Frankly my dear, the clothes you wear have always astounded me! They show no courage whatsoever!"

She gestured at me and said, "They are appallingly utilitarian. Gray, brown, navy blue, black clothes do nothing to bring out your odd but charming personality or your lack of gravity. You are a bit of a fluff, you know."

She wrinkled her nose in disdain and continued.

"Why don't you be brave and design some nice clothing for yourself? Something more feminine? Surely you can find something more comfortable and cooler than what you're wearing!"

She looked me up and down.

"Design something lightweight and colorful and I'll find someone to make it up for you...hmmm....come to think of it, I know an excellent dressmaker."

Sullenly, I shook my head no.

She became impatient with me.

"Stop being so dreary!" she shouted.

"It's not the end of the world!"

"It is to me!" I shouted back.

She ignored my words and eyed me, hands on her hips.

"Surely there are going to be some occasions when you will need to wear a nice attractive outfit!"

She laid her shears down and took a step towards me. Her eyes narrowed speculatively.

"Why don't you design...umm...some kind of ..." she waved her hands around "...leotard in a lightweight material to wear under your clothes? To cover the lines? You know, something like ballerinas wear? Maybe a thin body leotard that covers to wrists, ankles and neck?" She warmed to her subject. "Yes! That's it!"

I squinted at her. Wearing anything frilly or colorful would just draw more attention to me. And, one of the important ways I stayed hidden and protected was by wearing the plain "utility" clothing Aunt Amelia disdained.

Did she think I was a fool? I knew nothing about design. What was it with these women? The Shaman women wanted me to paint when I didn't know how, and now Aunt Amelia wanted me to design clothes, which I had no clue how to do. There was some kind of weird concept behind their thinking when it came to me that I just couldn't grasp. After a minute, I grudgingly nodded at her. If she wasn't going to fix the problem for me, I would just have to cover it up for now.

She rushed us off to shop for design supplies. We returned and spread them out. I laid down on a large piece of paper we taped together. Aunt Amelia traced my outline on it.

She was excited by "our adventure." That's what she called it. We shopped fabric stores. There were so many fabrics and variations on colors, it simply boggled the mind. We never knew there was a reason for creating a particular color! At times it was too much; we quit and went home to digest it.

Aunt Amelia took my measurements. We sketched the first leotard on paper. Then we matched it to a fabric, and she sent it off to the dressmaker.

By the time the third leotard came back, most of the glitches were ironed out. I ordered leotards in dark brown, navy, and black, but Aunt Amelia wasn't satisfied.

"Why do you keep picking those dark, somber colors when they are just the opposite of your personality? A court jester should never wear drab colors."

She eyed my halo of orange hair, the freckled, creamy skin that never wrinkled and my plump, defiant little figure.

"Have a little more spirit about yourself! You should take advantage of the leotards. Present yourself to people in a way that matches the lines you carry beneath them. Like a Sun Dancer does after Sun Dance is over. You went through those initiations, you earned those lines, so be proud of them! Show off your courage!"

"Ha!" I scoffed at the idea. She frowned and tapped her long, lean foot on the floor.

"Maybe you should retire to a nunnery. You know, a place where you can cover your body with a heavy black blanket and wear a piece of white sheet across your forehead and run around mumbling over a cross or something! That would be a real spiritual paradise for you, wouldn't it?"

She laughed at the expression on my face.

"We are going to visit a local store that carries a large supply of things we need."

In the store, she held up colorful trims against the neckline and sleeves of the leotard I was wearing. When I started my usual ritual of protest, she gave me a long, cool look and whispered in my ear.

"The animals you have on you are living beings. You keep forgetting that. They need to be honored by you. If you ever want to get out of your predicament, stop acting like a child throwing a temper tantrum and grow up!"

She turned and stalked out of the store. I stared after her, frozen in my tracks. She'd had enough. And she was absolutely right, I was acting like a brat.

"Aunt Amelia!" I yelled and ran after her. In that moment, I realized that I absolutely adored her and wouldn't fight her any more. I rushed out of the store and apologized.

She accepted my apology. Arm in arm, we went back in and picked out trims to edge the body leotards at the neck, wrist and ankle. At one point, she picked up a darling tiny, sequined blue fish. She dangled it in front of me and whispered, "It seems to me that if you need to be brave, you've been given a fabulous opportunity to do it right out in the open! Just flaunt your clothing! Add this little fish to represent the hidden animals. Or add other animal trims representing an attribute you are trying to develop! We should never stop learning, you know."

"Embellishments!"

We became fond of shouting the word together and laughing. Our imaginations blossomed. Soon there were silver butterflies, sequined fish and other animals on leotards, belts, scarves, and shoes. A creative part of me was awake, thanks to Aunt Amelia and the Shaman women. I didn't understand who I was any more, but who I was before never enjoyed life like I did now.

At Aunt Amelia's urging, I began designing simple tunics to go with the leotards. She said the tunics would fit my short, ample curves better than a dress. Tunics would make my eccentric outfits look as though I wore them that way on purpose.

"They will make you look more sophisticated and less childish. You don't want to look childish, do you? You're too old, and it isn't a position of power. Heck, you might end up looking like a dignified Pope, or maybe the high priestess of a jungle tribe in tunics."

We laughed. Then she sobered and said, "The point is, you need a way to display your dignity so people won't laugh at you, because they will certainly always notice you. If you want to be taken seriously, you'll have to work at it."

She studied my halo of orange hair with one hand on her hip and shook her head. "There's got to be a better way! Between your hair and makeup, you look like an orange with lips!"

"At least I don't look like a retired follies star!"

Aunt Amelia rolled her eyes heavenward.

"Are you saying I do?" she asked hopefully.

"Well, sort of," I said.

"Oooooh...I hope so!"

She laughed her great purple laugh and I couldn't help but join in.

I colored and cut my own hair. Every time Aunt Amelia tried to help me, the lines glowed and rushed up my face to seek her touch. She wasn't good at it anyway. In a salon, if someone touched me and the lines rose and they saw them, it would have caused an incident, so I colored it myself. I didn't think it turned out so bad each time. After all, variety is the spice of life.

We worked and played, and Auntie stayed pleased with me. I gladly took the suggestions she offered. We kept busy gardening, sailing, shopping and designing. We were enjoying life. Time passed swiftly. All of our undertakings finally wore Aunt Amelia out, and she began resting a lot while I took over our projects.

Outstandingly lovely dresses of peau de soie are never forgotten by their wearers. Many photo albums are necessary.

Chapter 21.   Aunt Amelia Leaves

Early one afternoon, I was sitting under a shade tree on the lawn trying to read a book, but I couldn't concentrate. I stared off in the distance, feeling sad for some reason. Something was nagging at me lately, but I couldn't quite put my finger on it. I sighed, laid the book down and stared across the lawn at the house. I kept doing that lately. Something about it was troubling me. Was it the architecture? No, it was beautiful. Still, while looking at it, I felt a sense of impending doom I couldn't shrug off or explain.

I was alone because Aunt Amelia was "resting" again. That's what she called it. I frowned down at the book. In fact, she was resting all the time these days. In that instant, I realized something was very wrong. She was too quiet and pale lately, and I was too busy to notice! I jumped up and hurried across the lawn. It seemed to take forever! I rushed into the house and ran upstairs to her room. I feared she was sleeping, so I opened her bedroom door and slipped in quietly.

She was sitting in a wingback chair by the window, gazing out across her gardens. I didn't want her to know what I was beginning to surmise, so I strolled innocently across the room and sat down in a chair near her.

Warm, fragrant air carried the smell of fresh cut grass through the open windows. I didn't speak, but as always, she could see right through my pretenses. I felt my chin tremble. I reached over and took her hand in mine. It felt warm and solid, large and comforting. I sighed sadly and dropped my head. Instantly I realized what I was doing, raised my head, and pasted a bright smile on my face.

"You should try that caricature with bright red lipstick instead of orange!"

She laughed at me.

"What's the matter with you now?"

I blurted.

"I'm so worried about you! You are spending so much time up here .... Resting?..." I gestured around the bedroom. "...dearest Aunt."

She cut off my words.

"I'm just a little under the weather. Now don't let yourself get all upset. You have such an imagination, you know! I have never seen anything like it."

I clung to her hand and kissed her palm.

"Yes, it is best to forget about it. We'll plan new things to do together as soon as you feel better. I don't have anyone else...you're the only one I have in the..." I flung a hand out to indicate the world.

But she didn't get better. The doctor began coming more frequently to the house to attend her. She refused to let me stay in the room with them. One morning, I cornered the doctor on my own.

"Would you walk with me in the garden?"

We went away from the house until we stood behind the veil of a flowering tree. The old, white-haired doctor took my hands and looked down into my eyes.

"She doesn't have very long, my dear," he announced soberly.

"You're the apple of her eye. She dotes on you, and you must do nothing to upset her. Especially do not talk to her about this."

My world fell apart at his words.

"You must do everything possible to make her comfortable and happy, for she has no other family she has ever been willing to claim."

He must have known how I felt, for the last thing he said was I shouldn't get too upset, Aunt Amelia was taking it very well, better than most of his other patients did.

She saw that I knew. She laughed at me and said she was prepared to go. Over the next few weeks, two Shaman women came to stay with her. They bore a haughty, regal, proud bearing, much like the Shaman women from the island. She said they were part of the island group, one in which she held lifelong membership.

"You should pay attention and learn what you can from them."

I shuddered.

"No way!"

She laughed and said, "Life is a classroom. We are all students of Life, but many people never make it past kindergarten!"

As Aunt Amelia's life ebbed away, she stayed cloistered with the mysterious, powerful women. They kept me informed of her condition in short, unsentimental sentences. I hired a woman to cook for them and another one to be at their beck and call for whatever they needed. Meanwhile, I hovered nervously at the edge of the sad situation.

*

Aunt Amelia said she wanted to be buried in the family plot beside her sweetheart, "Master Ronald B. Alderman." She insisted on a private memorial with only me and the two Shaman women.

After the funeral, the women quickly packed up and left. I never saw them again. I wandered through the house and grounds, listless, sad, and lost. My sorrow was terrible and deep. Aunt Amelia was my best friend and mentor. I loved her greatly. I found myself pacing endlessly through the big empty house and garden. I went down to the beach and stared at her little sailboat for hours on end.

*

A few weeks later, when her will was read, I expected to be thrown out. Instead, I was left a wealthy woman. I knew she was well off financially, but I never knew the extent of it.

At first I kept the daily routine we'd followed, but it was meaningless without her. The huge, empty house rang with fond memories and my anguish as I paced restlessly through it. She had been my only true companion. I would never forget her and the way she changed my life. She knew all my secrets and who I was before I knew it myself.

I rubbed my arms. The glowing lines moved restlessly. Aunt Amelia had been the instigator, the rudder and the creator of the impossible, remarkable journey I was on. She had sent me out on quest. With her, I knew I could make it, but without her, could I? My soul would miss her always and forever; she had set me on a journey of self-discovery, proudly and exotically dressed in colorful leotards bearing sequins, birds and animals.

I designed more body leotards. As I worked, I thought of Aunt Amelia. To honor her wisdom, I chose soft, vibrant colors in assorted lightweight textures. I asked the dressmaker to add sprinkles of gemstones to all the edges.

Then I designed a new tunic with belled, beige sleeves and little brown sparrows flying endlessly across it, and a snow white, silver edged body leotard to go under it. I wore it to Aunt Amelia's grave, then took it off and laid it on top of her grave for the sparrows to protect her.

One night I dreamed of the animal lines on my body. They were set free; they ran freely and boldly across leotards and tunics in incredible colors and lines. Tiny animals and trims danced and pranced right along with them on the edges of leotards. I woke up and hurried to the drawing table while the images were still fresh.

I worked for days. When I finished, there were sixteen animal designs stacked on the drawing table, one for every animal tattooed on me.

I sent the designs off with instructions to the dressmaker. She exclaimed.

"Where do you get these marvelous ideas?"

"I guess I have a good imagination."

The day came when sixteen beautiful body leotards and matching tunics were spread out on tables, each one in a clear, gorgeous color, with a large outline of an animal running across it! The lines on my body hummed with appreciation. For once the picky things were happy with something I did.

A thought occurred to me. Why not design ritual dresses for the Shaman women? After all, I wouldn't be whatever I was now without them. After all, they'd led me to a new place in life that both astounded and filled me with awe daily.

*

I ran upstairs and searched through Aunt Amelia's papers until I found her address book. I designed the ritual dresses, bought the materials and trims, and sent them off to the dressmaker. When they came back, I sent them to the island.

I wandered the grounds and took care of odds and ends. I took pictures of Aunt Amelia and her fiancé to the cemetery. I placed his picture on her grave, then her picture on his grave. I sat down and looked at the two graves and read to them.

"Once up on a time there was a pair of sweethearts who inhabited the Earth boldly with grace and a little cussing now and then.

They met and loved each other beyond the pale instantly. Theirs was not a simple love. It was complex, strong, and intelligent. The kind of love that never ends no matter what happens. Yes, the two sweethearts were destined to be together, but not right then. They would have to wait because, you see, Fate was on the move. Providence declared that the man go ahead of his true love to make a comfortable place for her in the unseen world.

She was bereft when the jealousy of an old boyfriend delivered her darling beyond the pale, but she was a woman who understood many things. She was a realist. She knew karma was at work for a higher purpose. At last the time came for her to meet her sweetheart again. He was a fine provider, as she discovered after she met him there, so she settled in and lived in beauty, plenty, and love happily ever after with him. The end."

*

It was time to move on. I had Aunt Amelia's suite of rooms cleaned and closed up and her little sailboat put in dry dock. Instinctively, I knew I would come back here someday. I contacted my children. They were stiff with me but doing well. Everyone was in good health. I sent them modest checks with a polite note. Then I closed up Aunt Amelia's house and left. It was done. I was on my own again.

Now I honored my animal tattoos instead of viewing them as living nightmares. Now their beauty was tastefully and discreetly covered with fine clothing instead of anger, astonishment and shame.

But I still had to pet them plenty. Rub, rub, rub so they wouldn't get a rash or send a hot flash to fry my ass when they got pissed off at me for neglecting them. Spoiled brats! Couldn't go to a doctor. They knew it, too. So I rubbed, massaged and petted. I bought gallons of expensive organic, unscented, all natural, bio-degradable body lotion at their insistence and used up a lot of ice to get me through learning their ways. Good thing Aunt Amelia left me the money to do it with.

Pique has many desirable qualities. Some must be searched out.

Ćhapter 22. The Hawk and the Old Woman in the Moon

Melanie watched the huge brown and red hawk swoop down. It perched in the tall pine tree close to the front porch. The hawk took up residence in the tree with the coming of the first snow. The snow quickly melted and the weather changed back into late fall, but the hawk stayed. She stepped through the door. The hawk lifted in the air and flew a short distance away to another tree. She shaded her eyes and stared up at it. It stared back at her with black, knowing eyes.

*

Since Melanie believes in omens and signs, I pretended I didn't notice the huge, predatory hawk, but of course, she pointed it out to me.

"What do you think it's after?"

The hawk fixed a fierce, predatory, baleful glare on me. I looked into its eyes and saw a mirror of everything I was ever afraid of. I was in trouble again. I froze in fear. Melanie took my arm.

"Let's go in the house. I'll make tea."

We went inside. I made an effort at conversation. I asked a few questions about her extended trip. I didn't want her to know how much I missed her, or how much seeing the hawk had affected me.

In a short time, I excused myself and headed home. The hawk flew close to me and screamed, letting me know it was following me with a purpose. I felt the lines of the hawk on my right shoulder moving in answer to the hawk's scream. The hawk circled Windbay Cottage, then flew into the back yard. I opened the door and ran inside.

I cleared a space on a low table in the living room; placed thick white candles on it. I lit them to honor the Shaman women who brought the hawk to me by placing its living lines on my body. With the candles lit, the "hawk" became the Hawk with a capital H.

I sighed. I was damn tired of being leery, of having to go through major, unexpected interruptions in my life. No doubt they were making me even more elderly and insane. And, how could I ever have a relationship with anybody with all of this going on? What would we talk about? I meant Lucian in particular.

I changed into a black leotard and tunic and applied bright red lipstick so it would look like I was planning to go to a party just in case this was my demise. I lay down on my bed and thought about Melanie. She was full bodied, deep red wine, a smooth vitality poured out with graceful sensibility on all those around her. Lucian was black onyx, steady, dark and cool, mother of pearl with hidden depths. Calm, soothing, dark water smoothing its path under a bridge dappled with sunlight. I wished I was with them and not here alone, shivering in fear of what was coming.

*

I fell asleep. I dreamed I was standing in a summer meadow watching the flower stalks around me swaying in a warm breeze. Tiny and scared, I stared up in fear as the huge Hawk swooped down, swept me up in its grip and bore me swiftly away. I hung from the Hawk's grip, limp and dangling. I was a tiny two dimensional being, like a flat piece of paper on a kite string, hanging beneath the Hawk's mighty breast. I smelled the woody, bird smell of the Hawk. Warmth emanated from its body, rushing out in steady circles. The wind from the Hawk's wings rushing over me felt good. The sound of the Hawk's wings moving through the air was comforting.

I lolled beneath the Hawk, enjoying the ride. Nothing mattered. I wasn't worried about anything. Then the Hawk flew over a lush green meadow, and dropped me. I mouthed a silent scream of horror as I plummeted towards the green, grass covered Earth below.

I hit the earth and fell deep into it but sprang right back up from inside the hole I made. I stood on the Earth in the wind and grew taller and taller. A sharp, curved beak formed on my face. I screamed with the fierce power of the Hawk. I flapped my arms and my wings grew bigger and wider. Then I flew. Up into the sky effortlessly, higher and higher, until I was just a speck in the universe. I flew in tireless night flight over the continents of the Earth. In familiar places, I saw people of long ago Earth staring up at me, knowing I was up there. Their small oval faces glowed fearfully up at me from around their fires.

The people below were white or red or yellow or dark as the midnight sun. I heard their rhythms and felt their hands beating on drums. Those ones knew me. They were familiar with the Shadow fear carries. I saw it in their eyes. I watched my Shadow fall over many creatures, frightening them. They ran and hid. It didn't matter to me. It was just the way of nature until I needed to eat.

I flew and soared and glided a long time. I felt the fragile, hollow bones in my sharp, pointed breast, and how strong and fast my heart beat. I felt the remains of a mouse in my stomach and how my body juices were digesting it. The mouse was rich and gave my blood strength.

My nest called me home. I flew over it, circled and landed. The twigs I used to make it with were short, thin, and hard, but I knew how to settle into them. I sank down into my nest and slept. I was content with what life brought me. I was alone in a high place where the wind blew, and it didn't matter. I was alone and not alone, no longing in me except for tomorrow's hunt.

*

A bright light shining in my eyes woke me. The moon was shining through the bedroom window, bathing me in loud, insistent light, calling me to come out. I stumbled to the bathroom and looked in the mirror at my right shoulder. The glowing lines of the Hawk were racing around.

Well, I guessed I wasn't going to die inside Windbay Cottage, which would have been more convenient for me; nobody seemed to care about that, so I changed clothes and reapplied fresh red lipstick for courage. I went out the back door to find the Hawk. The air was cold, crisp and clear. The Hawk lifted up and circled the yard. It would not leave until its business with me was done. It flew high, looking like a tiny speck in the sky. The hawk tattoo on my shoulder moved restlessly.

I stared up at the Old Moon. She looked haggard and ancient and stripped of clouds. She looked irritated and damn tired. She rode high in the sky, filled with impatient, bright white light, waiting for me.

I ran back in the house and slapped my leftover hot chocolate on the stove to heat while I mixed a ball of rich tallow from the things I stocked for the bird feeder out back.

I wrapped the ball in foil and shoved it in my coat pocket. I gulped down the warm cocoa. At least I would have chocolate before I possibly died. I hurried out into the cold night, heading for the quaint little park on the edge of the village.

The hour was late. It was freezing. A bitter wind was blowing. The park was bare and empty. I sat down at a picnic table and waited for the hawk. I might live and I might die tonight, but the Hawk with a capital H must have its way because of the initiations that were set in motion on the island. There was no turning back.

The wind tugged at my muffler. I waited, scared, cold and alone in the dark. Finally the Hawk landed near the picnic table. I reached in my pocket and took out the large ball of rich tallow. Slowly and carefully, without making any sudden moves, I pulled the foil away from it and placed it in my open hand, palm up. I watched the Hawk out of the corner of my eye. I knew better than to look directly at it. The Hawk stared at me with piercing eyes. It moved closer. I sat as still as I could, yet I couldn't help quaking with spasms of cold and terror.

The voice of the Old Woman in the Moon called down to me. I looked up at her. She held my eyes and ordered me to keep them fixed on her. I did not dare look away from the Old Woman in the Moon. I was glad she was there for me to look to.

The Hawk's fierce claws made scratching sounds as it came to my hand. I felt its beak jerking at the rich tallow. I raised my arm involuntarily when the Hawk stepped on the right wrist of my coat and began working its way up to my right shoulder.

The Hawk screamed. My ears rang with the piercing sound, but I managed to stay still and keep my arm braced on the table while I stared up at the Old Woman in the Moon.

I felt the Hawk's feet biting through my coat as it sought purchase on its way up to my shoulder. It ripped and tore away the cloth at the shoulder of my coat until it reached the bare skin glowing with moving lines.

The Hawk screamed again. I clenched my jaws and managed to hold steady while it jerked and ripped out my old, ragged, empty, worn out courage, and tossed it away. When it was done, the Hawk hopped back down on the table. It looked around and gave a harsh cry, then flew to the ground a few feet away. I watched it walk in a circle and preen until it was cleansed of the old stuff it tore away from me. Then it took back to the night sky. I watched it circle higher and higher until it was out of sight.

I looked around in a daze. It was still dark and very cold. The Moon was gone. I didn't know when she left. I pulled my coat close and headed home, stumbled into Windbay Cottage and fell straight into bed.

The next morning, I showered away the bits of dried blood the Hawk with a capital H left on my right shoulder, doctored the scratches, and drifted off to bed, expecting to sleep the relieved, innocent sleep of someone who just ended a horrible ordeal and needed at least three months of bed rest to recover. Maybe room service too.

Not so.

The Hawk's fun was just beginning. It came to me again in my sleep. Once more I fell into the darkness beneath its wings. But this time I was far from being a relaxed puppet. This time, I cowered in the shadows of the huge wings above me, reliving each time I was cruel to someone out of fear and ignorance, reliving in excruciating detail each time I was crude, angry, mean, or arrogant. I relived blustering around, acting like I knew what I was doing, when I was secretly terrified of everything, but stubbornly refused to admit it. I recalled each person I turned my back on, and all the times I was shortsighted, resented others or ran away. The list was long. As I mourned the endless stream of mistakes I had made, I began to fear for my soul. How had this happened without my intending it? Who really ran my life?

Days went by in the terrible darkness beneath the Hawk's wings with the Old Woman in the Moon screaming at me and the Hawk beating its huge wings to stir the karmic memories.

I walked the floor and recapitulated my wrongs. I couldn't reconcile any part of my life. There was no going back, no explaining, no redemption possible. Hell, I was old. Some of them were dead and didn't give a damn anyway. Others were alive and didn't give a damn. I was a failure as a human being. My soul started to wilt.

Late one night, I realized I would have to die, and I accepted it. I got in bed and stared out the window at the dark night outside. I gladly released my soul to its flight into the darkness. It would go wherever it had to go. At least the miserable memories of all my wrongs would end now.

*

I woke up the next morning in this world, in this same place. I figured on waking up in hell, but something was different. I looked around the bedroom, puzzled.

The Dove

I thought about the materials Aunt Amelia and I once looked at in the stores and remembered crepe, and what Aunt Amelia said about it.

"Crepe is a mild material, a covering suited for removal only when the presence of doves is required so angels of peace can descend."

I felt something move in my chest and looked down. A white Dove was settled there. Did Aunt Amelia send it? I looked closer. The Dove had made a nest beside the fierce Hawk. They were sitting there together, in my chest, side by side, solemn and hopeful. I stared at them, and they stared back at me.

Days passed. Little by little, the Dove and the Hawk formed an uneasy truce. The Hawk had been alone for a long time and it was lonely. It did not try to kill or drive the Dove away, though it could have. It had gained wisdom and realized that the price would be too high for its soul to pay if it drove the Dove away. It was glad for company of any kind.

The Old Woman in the Moon came and scolded me. She told me I didn't get to lay around on my powder puff designer ass. She reminded me of the Venerable Hare's power, of the clock ticking Time away, and ordered me to get my sorry ass out of bed, to stop whining and get to work. She called me a sniveling lazy ass.

So it was that I began my first Spirit Weaving job without union representation, with the Venerable Hare knitting together the dappled Light and Shadow that lay between the Hawk and the Dove. I wove sorrow and redemption together, like the Rabbit and the Venerable Hare, and as I realized what I was really doing, I sobbed through the work of it.

The Old Woman in the Moon told me to stop being such a crybaby; there was no overtime, insurance, workers comp or mandatory coffee breaks, so suck it up; she ordered me to get over myself. She said there were millions of kinds of spiritual work going on all the time everywhere and I had just answered a want ad for spiritual employment, so I better dry up, or I could get my sorry ass fired. Yes, I did have to put in overtime, and no, I didn't get paid time and a half.

"Big Deal!" she told me. "Get over thinking spiritual work is just for elite, evolving souls. That's elevator thinking. It's everybody's gig."

While I was learning spiritual weaving, I started wondering what my family had gone through. I wondered what they lost and what their karma was. I was never able to give them what their spirits needed. Now I understood whose job that was, and always was.

A Higher Power was at work throughout all of life, call it Spirit, God, Jesus, Buddha, Whatever. It was the Boss. I was to forgive myself for having human limits and only do what I could. What I could do was my job. My forty hour week. I could vacation the rest of the time. Sure. Yeah. Right.

When the Old Woman in the Moon was satisfied that I had begun to understand, she left me to it with a word or two of sage advice.

"Okay, dumbass, I'm taking off now. Don't get in trouble or I'll be back. Get it?"

I nodded fearfully.

The days sped by as I understood more. I ate whatever was handy, slept and walked the floor while little chinks of sunlight started shining in my Being. I wove us together, me and the Hawk and the Dove, and we began working together.

One day I felt finished. I felt light. I didn't hurt. I looked at my skin. The lines of the Hawk and the Dove and the Old Woman in the Moon were gone. The sunlight was returned to my life, but I needed to be careful of it for I sunburned easily.

I understood now that I owed a debt to my children and family, but there were many things that I didn't owe them, things only

Spirit could take care of, for they and I had been living other lives long before we came together in this lifetime. Our karmic paths were different. We each had our own Spirit path to walk with a far older family of unseen advisors than just our current mother and father.

I did have some things I wanted to do for them if they would let me, though. I needed to be a part of their lives again. It would take time to find ways to do it, but I was an Old Moon Woman now with a Hawk's courage and a Dove's compassion. Now I could figure it out.

I went to the kitchen. The cupboards were bare. I was seriously hungry. I showered and dressed in clean clothes. My face looked slimmer in the mirror. The color was completely gone from my hair, but the good news was that it looked like I'd lost some weight during this latest ordeal.

My hair was a short white cloud that looked like it was trying to help me think better. I draped a floral scarf over it, tied it at my nape, and applied bright pink lipstick. I would color my hair later.

Right now, eating was the top priority. It was time to go back out into the world. I planned to start with a huge, delectable meal at the village teashop.

Fleece is warm as a lamb and comforting as a mother's touch.

Chapter 23. Love's Search

Melanie knocked hard on Avalon's door. Still no answer. She was worried. She asked around the village but no one else had seen her. Melanie remembered the hawk. She hadn't seen Avalon in weeks. She wondered if the Hawk had anything to do with her disappearance. She turned and hurried down the sidewalk.

*

A worried frown crossed Lucian's face at Melanie's last words, "I can't imagine where she is..." Her voice trailed off as Lucian rushed into the hall. She watched him yank on a coat with swift, precise movements, sit down and jerk on his boots. She followed him as he rushed out the door. A short time later she watched him pound on Avalon's door.

She'd never seen him act like this. She grinned involuntarily. In some ways, she found it interesting to observe this new facet of his gloomy, isolated, intense nature.

An old fisherman in coveralls strolled by. He stopped and shook his grizzled head.

"Won't do ya' naw' good," he said. Melanie watched Lucian's jaw working with the effort to control his temper.

"Why not?" Lucian asked him softly.

"'Cause she's up to the tea shop."

Lucian scowled and rushed past the man. He grabbed Melanie's arm and hurried her down the sidewalk. She ran to keep up with him. He stared straight ahead, his face a dark thunderstorm.

They came to an abrupt stop in front of the tea shop. He jerked the door open and rushed inside. Melanie followed. People sat around small, dainty tables and in the large, sturdy booths in the back of the tea shop, drinking tea, leisurely eating pastries.

Melanie watched Lucian's eyes search for Avalon. The look in them reminded her of the hawk's eyes. He saw her. She was sitting in a back-corner booth. He let out a deep breath and turned to Melanie.

"You go ahead," he said, "I have to use the bathroom."

She smirked at him. She knew he was giving himself time to calm down. He would go in there and scowl at himself in the mirror, mutter a bunch of cuss words, then come back out all smooth and distant. He scowled at her and turned away.

Melanie threaded her way between the tiny tables and chairs until she stood in front of

Avalon. Avalon was lost in thought. She sat in the booth, holding a mug of tea in both hands, absently sipping it. She was wearing a long pink coat with bloody rips in the right shoulder.

Avalon blinked and gave her a slow, timid smile. Melanie saw the tender rawness and the tiredness behind the smile. She slid into the other side of the booth.

"Lucian is with me," she announced. Avalon stared blankly at her. Before Melanie could speak again, Lucian planted himself in front of the booth, a large, black monolith glaring down at Avalon. She didn't notice his glare of disapproval. He slid into the booth on Melanie's side, not taking his eyes off Avalon.

His eyes roamed over her again and again, picking up every nuance. Her pink coat. There were blood stained rips and ragged tears at the shoulder. His eyes moved to her face. He noted the tiredness and the newness shadowing her eyes. A kind of flowered scarf thing was tied over her hair. He sighed. Women did the oddest things to themselves! He looked closer. Her face and sharp little chin were pale. Her rosebud mouth trembled beneath a slash of florescent pink lipstick.

She looked thinner and older and haggard and brand new, all at the same time. Sort of like a new penny, if only he could see her hair to confirm its usual color.

He wanted to get out of the dainty, too-small booth, pull her out of the other side of it, and fold her in his arms to protect her. She didn't notice his intense examination. She didn't notice anything.

The waitress came to take their order. Melanie started to order but Lucian interrupted, and ordered for all of them. Melanie grinned and sat back. In a stern voice that brooked no argument, Lucian ordered three glasses of ice water, three hot chocolates, a bunch of pastries, and three huge sandwiches with fresh chips and slaw on the side.

"And bring fresh coffee!" he commanded. The waitress rushed away. He turned back to Avalon.

"If they sold coats here, I would buy you a new one right now."

Melanie snickered behind her hand. He glared at her. She made big innocent eyes back at him.

Avalon flinched at the challenging sound in his voice. Her hand flew to the torn right shoulder of her pink coat. She tugged at the rips, trying to pull them together. Realizing she couldn't fix it, she gave up, slid out of the booth, wiggled out of the coat with the finesse of a contortionist, and hung the coat on the large coat hook at the end of the booth.

Lucian was staring at her in mute wonder. Again. Patiently she stood still and waited. What was it with people always staring at her? She watched his head bobbing back and forth, up and down.

She smoothed the bright pink fuzzy sweater that ended just above her knees. Her scarf. Did it still cover her hair? She reached up to check it.

Lucian listened to the silky whisper of the short, blue plaid skirt ending just below her knees. Rhinestones edged the neckline, wrists and ankles of the dark purple leotard she wore beneath it all.

"So, we've got hot pink and purple with rhinestones, and a blue plaid skirt, and some kind of flowered thing over her hair. What about her shoes?" he muttered to himself. Involuntarily he looked down with dread, then sighed in relief. She was wearing plain navy blue flats.

Avalon waited while he muttered to himself like the first time they met, but this time she had an answer for him.

"I keep trying to get my life to settle into one long, drawn out day of solid anguish, so I can have an excuse to wear the daily assortment of utility gray I used to, but it keeps turning out this way!"

She spoke softly and blinked woefully. His original surge of protective compassion left him hanging in the lurch as he gaped at her. He couldn't help himself. He burst out laughing. She grinned at him and vamped for a moment.

He couldn't stop staring at Avalon Blue... spelled B-L-U-E. He felt warmth creep in and out of his face. He didn't know what to think of her. She escaped every category. She was an orphan, a waif, a lost old woman and a conjurer. She was too young for her age, naïve, ditsy, courageously following her own path.

Her hair was a different shade of orange every time he saw her, or it was covered with some weird cloth. Her clothes belonged on someone who lived on the moon and posed atop a confectioner's elaborate creation.

He sensed that she was sad and intense and private, and no doubt laughed as openly and fatally as the moon. He wanted to protect her and laugh with her and hold her. Slowly it dawned on him that he wanted to keep her around for a long time. He was astounded.

They stared at each other. The silence thickened. Melanie watched them. Not many people could hold Lucian's intense stare like Avalon was doing. But the staring went on and on, and Melanie began to feel ignored, unseen, an unwanted old relic, ancient, gray-haired, with either arthritis or lumbago building up, one of those aging ailments.

She elbowed Lucian out of the booth, stood up and grabbed her purse.

"I have to run some errands. I'm sure you'll both miss me very much! I'll be back soon."

In their condition, she doubted they heard a word she said, but she did her duty and informed them anyway. She stopped on the sidewalk in front of the tearoom to dance a couple steps. They had it bad! She'd never seen Lucian like this! Well, it was high time! She felt relief. Maybe he would learn to grin or even crack a tiny smile? Probably not, she decided after thinking about it. The odds were definitely against it.

She wondered how Avalon was going to handle the heavy weight of Lucian's solemn love. She suspected he would want to manage, protect and hover over all of Avalon's doings and monitor every breath she took. She laughed and skipped down the street.

*

After running all the silly little errands she could think of, she returned to the tea shop. Lucian was holding Avalon's hand in a death grip. The food was cold, limp, untouched.

Her return broke the spell between them. Lucian reluctantly slid his hand back from Avalon's and she slid out of the booth. He helped her put on her coat. She looked up at him.

"I have to go home now," she announced, like a prim little schoolgirl.

Lucian took her arm. "I'll walk you home!" he commanded in a deep voice. Then he remembered Melanie and amended his words to include her.

"Oh! And you, too!"

Melanie watched Lucian lead Avalon by the hand out the door of the tea shop, as though he was leading her onto a ballroom dance floor, but without paying the bill. The shop-keeper ran after him to collect his money. Lucian looked dazed, like he'd walked into a wall. Avalon didn't notice anything.

She followed along behind them, keeping her face straight. She waited on the sidewalk while Lucian walked Avalon to her door. He grabbed the key out of her hand and unlocked the door for her.

Then Avalon looked up at him and Melanie watched him slowly fall apart. He gathered Avalon in his arms and rocked her back and forth and lectured her for hiding from them and wouldn't let her answer.

Tears gathered in Melanie's eyes as she watched the lovely, somber man who had too little laughter in his life. She observed the flash of white at his temples and the leanness of his body and the extreme craving emanating from him. She noted the soft, plump curves of the little woman he held and her natural acceptance of him just as he was. Avalon stayed melted into his arms, vital and nestled and open, in total acceptance of his fierce embrace and scolding words. Melanie wiped her eyes and walked a few steps away to give them privacy.

At last Lucian let Avalon go. She slipped inside her house. Melanie watched as he lurched down the sidewalk like a man walking close to deadly quicksand. She took his arm and led him home. She gave him a brief hug and hurried home. There was definitely more research to do!

Jacquard can be a magical weave.

Çhapter 24. The Circus is in Town!

The Squirrel, the Mouse and the Crow

A squirrel, a mouse and a crow have been busy harvesting for winter in the yard and trees of Windbay Cottage. They noisily race through trees and over ground, keeping their busy-ness in my face. I don't care. I watch them work while I play. Like the grasshopper in the story, I can't commit to anything.

Lucian is carefully distant with me since the day in the tea shop. I suspect he is waiting for a further indication of affection from me. I yearn to offer him a finished and complete me, but I can't. I don't know what else to do, so I play.

Sometimes the Squirrel, Mouse, and Crow pile stuff against my front door. They watch me with bright, knowing eyes. They can't fool me. I know they are trying to get a message across, but I ignore them and keep on playing.

Curiosity got the best of me one day. I picked up a scrap of shiny paper propped against the front door. The paper looked like a carnival or a circus advertisement. It read "Come Join the Fun!" in bold red letters on a gold foil background. I taped it to the window beside the front door to let the three varmints know I was paying attention.

They left more shiny gold and red scraps up against the door with things written on them like "Watch Waldo the Magician Perform Astounding Feats of Magic!" and "Ride the Silver Airplanes!" I taped them up beside the first scrap, and went back to playing.

*

Lucian invited Melanie and me to dinner. I arrived early. Lucian opened the door. I sucked in my breath and stared him up and down. He looked like a handsome pirate in his dark suit with a red rose in his lapel. I smiled up at him and waited while he inventoried my black tunic with tiny silver swans circling the hem, worn over a matching black leotard with tiny silver swans circling the wrist, neck and ankles. Black leather flats and matching purse completed the outfit.

I smiled up at him smugly, congratulating myself on my classy, conservative outfit. My hair was the many colors of a setting sun again; that, I couldn't do anything about.

"This is the house I saw from the beach at the See Shell Motel! I've wanted to see it ever since!" I exclaimed.

He smiled at me, white teeth even in his handsome face. I wondered if they were

216

dentures. He took my arm and we toured the house while waiting for Melanie. The tall, spacious rooms were elegant, filled with both local and European furnishings.

We stopped in front of the paintings of his mother and father in the gallery. He said he was an only child. His parents passed away years ago. I didn't ask how. Another time when we were closer, maybe. I learned that he traveled the world frequently on business but returned often to his childhood home.

He said Mrs. Bentley, the housekeeper, had been with the family since before time began; a girl would help her with dinner tonight. His speech was formal, polite and informative.

Dinner was served in the dining room closest to the kitchen for Mrs. Bentley's sake. We ate at a rustic wood table with low backed chairs. A small sideboard of the same wood took up half of one wall. A small table and two chairs were set by the windows overlooking the back yard. A pastoral painting of a country scene in a gilt frame hung above a small, lit fireplace. A small, simple chandelier over the table gave off soft light. Long windows draped in thin red silk overlooked an expanse of lawn bordered by the black wrought iron fence I'd seen from the beach.

We lingered after dinner. Lucian poured red wine and we drank to each other's health. He entertained us with stories of his mother and father and his adventures growing up in this house. His conclusion was that he inherited his mother's coloring, his father's build, and his personality from Mrs. Bentley.

Melanie entertained us with snippets of stories about raising her large, chaotic family.

They were careful not to ask me anything about myself. I felt both sad and relieved at their kindness, and found myself telling them about the Squirrel, the Mouse, and the Crow leaving me remnants of carnival bills on the porch.

Melanie cupped her chin in her hand and stared at me. She said, "Hmmm....No circus visits here. It's remote, you know... Just a small traveling carnival now and then...the kind with old, tarnished equipment, a bit of neon, and a lot of old worn out, though charming, children's rides..."

*

A few days later, Melanie, Lucian and I met at the bakery for lunch. We talked about the fall season.

I said, "This is apple cider time. I remember the red barns and the cider presses and the wonderful apple smell that soaked into the fiber of the barn boards. I remember the smells of hay curing in barn lofts, the cold, crisp taste of fresh apple juice pouring out of presses, and the fragrance of fermenting apple juice changing into hard cider."

Lucian said, "There's an apple orchard a couple hours away where they made cider the old-fashioned way. I can drive. We can spend the night at a bed and breakfast near the old cider mill!"

Next morning, he picked me up in a large black and silver car of some kind. When we were in the car, he handed me a small white box. Inside was a shiny silver pin.

"Oh!" I breathed in awe. I picked the delicate silver circle up and examined it. It was a miniature Ferris wheel with six tiny seats with tiny gemstones at the edge of each seat. Cunning, amazing, tiny little fish rode in each one of the seats.

"Lucian, it's absolutely stunning!"

I handed the elegant pin to him. He fastened it to my sweater, then gave me a swift peck on the cheek. He looked away and put the car into gear while I stared out the window, humming a mindless tune.

We picked Melanie up and wandered the back roads admiring the fall colors of field, farm and forest.

The bed and breakfast was a tall Victorian house loaded with gothic peaks and gables. It was dusty and filled with creepy noises. Lucian reserved rooms overlooking the farm and cider mill a short distance away. We climbed the creaky wood steps to the third floor. Lucian carried my suitcase into my room. I ran to the window, opened it, and stared out at the farm. I yearned for the barnyard and yeasty smells of feed and apples. I needed to hear the cattle lowing at dusk and the chickens clucking in the early morning. Lucian's voice interrupted my thoughts.

"Is the room adequate, Avalon?"

"Oh, yes!" I danced an impromptu jig.

"'Tis' the Irish in me," I explained to him, pitifully sighing and rolling my eyes. "We can dance a jig any time, any place."

I shook my head mournfully. "It's genetic."

"I have a confession to make.", Lucian said just as mournfully. He shook his head and sighed mightily.

"No one else would stay in the three rooms we've taken, so I got a good discount on them." He chuckled wickedly and rubbed his hands together, waiting for me to ask the inevitable question. I did.

"Why won't anyone stay in 'em?"

He assumed a mournful pose and sighed again. He said, "They are haunted by the original tenants of this house, Black Jack Donavan, a gambler with a peg leg and Elegant Smith, a card shark, of whom it was said she had a bitter mouth. They married, and she yearned to become a "landlubber" and raise little landlubbers in this house, but the Fates were against it. They sailed away and never returned, but their restless ghosts came back to haunt this house."

He grinned. "Yes. Tis' the pirate in me that booked them when I heard the story."

We settled in, then strolled to the apple farm together. We drank fresh cider and ate donuts. We petted the animals and strolled through the barns.

Lucian drove us to a nearby village for dinner. It was dusk when we reached the village. I heard faint strains of carnival music. Lucian and Melanie broke into pleased laughter at my look of wonder.

"Would you like to go to the carnival now or eat first?" they asked. I sucked in a breath of joy.

"Aha! You tricked me! Let's go to the carnival!"

The carnival was in a hay field on the edge of the village. We crossed the field and ducked under thin strands of brightly colored lights. The smell of popcorn and cotton candy, music and people laughing surrounded us. This was a place to forget our cares. We linked arms and sauntered along.

I was happy, but my good mood slipped away as an old grief rose up in me. I tried to ignore it. I didn't want them to see me like this.

Melanie and Lucian were playing a game at one of the booths. I hurried away, memories of the young girl I once was, flooding me. My family had gone to the carnival every fall. It was the happiest day of the year for each of us, a respite from the life we led.

I remembered my brother Harold buying a spool of cotton candy at the carnival. A young man, awkward in good clothes, his big, callused hands holding the white paper tube with the delicate, spun pink sugar wrapped around it so carefully! Something so light and sweet, something that couldn't last, something made of fairy tales and legends held tenderly in his large hands. I thought of his meanness when he was around people and his helpless rage that only faded when he was mending fences or milking cows. He was always working. I recalled seeing him picking daisies in the field, and later, seeing them in a fruit jar on the kitchen windowsill.

A smiling woman strolled past. In her smile, I saw my sister Greta's mouth soften from its tightly pursed grip into a small, thin, curve of pleasure. She smiled that same way the day her future husband gave her an engagement knot of field flowers to dry for their wedding.

I remembered watching my mother and sister's backs bent over the washboard while they exchanged bitter words about the never ending work-load. Back then, I heard only their words; I didn't understand them. Now in my mind's eye, I saw the curves of their tired backs and the wisps of hair that floated around their faces from the hot, steamy wash water. I watched them wipe away sweat with the backs of their red, raw hands.

My father always set his striped work cap on the kitchen table after work. It was his ritual. He was proud to own two work caps. I remembered the soft feather beds I fell asleep in while my father's voice retold the stories of the travels he took when he was young.

They had protected me from joining into the lives they lived. They kept me fed and tucked up in featherbeds and later, forced me out.

For the first time, I asked myself why. Maybe they didn't want or like me because I only added to the family misery. Just one more hopeless person caught up in poverty and helplessness.

Or maybe underneath it all, they hoped I might escape their fated poverty. And it seems I did. Had they not rejected me, I wouldn't have written to Aunt Amelia or be here now.

The Ferris wheel music caught my attention. I touched the pin Lucian gave me. Brother Tom loved Ferris wheels. He said riding one was the only time he'd ever get to see the world from a larger place. Now I understood what he meant.

I looked around with new eyes. The carnival was the only place my family and I were truly together. A place where we let each other have brief glimpses of each other's hopes and dreams without trying to destroy them. Each one of us, in whatever way, had found enough magic at the carnival to nourish our dreams through until the next carnival.

I wanted to cry. I was a woman past sixty who didn't know any more about my family than I did when I was a child, reading all those books. It was true, I had saved myself from the meanness, but the price was high.

Abruptly, I heard someone order me to stop sniveling. To get off my ass and do something about it before it was too late, before everybody died off. It sounded like Aunt Amelia's voice. I listened as she shoved the remembrance of the inheritance into my consciousness, like shoving a hope chest into a desperate spinster's barren bedroom.

I heard her words. "No inheritance is ever meant for just one. It affects all. Why do you think you came to me, Fluffy?"

Her voice faded. Suddenly I was filled with new purpose. I would pretend my family was here with me. Together, we would find the duck pond and choose a yellow duck for sister Greta, who always coveted an acre of land, and keep the prize for her. We would throw darts at balloons and win a vase for brother Harold to put the flowers of the fields in. We would watch Tom ride the Ferris wheel carrying binoculars.

I touched the Ferris wheel pin, vowing to find something like it to send to him.

My mother always wanted a pink refrigerator and a turquoise washer and dryer. And white lace curtains, pink cabbage flower wallpaper to paste wherever, and a maid to help her with the work so her daily life would be easier. My snippy, spiteful sister Dessie would get a sack of coins and jeweled hair combs. My father, a fancy train set, a Nubian goat, and a fine wood barrel to brew feed in.

I felt something nibbling at my toes. I looked down. A Squirrel, a Mouse and a Crow were gathered at my feet! I laughed.

"Your cousins are at home. Any messages to take back to them?"

They chattered at me, then scampered under a tent corner and disappeared.

*

The next morning I called down to the desk and ordered toast and juice. After a quick shower, I wrapped up in a thick, white robe. I heard a knock on the door and assumed it was room service.

"Come in!" I sang out.

Lucian opened the door and walked in. I froze. I couldn't take my eyes off him. He wore jeans and black riding boots. His white shirt was damp at the collar. My eyes ran up and down him as I slowly realized that he must have been out horseback riding.

He waited with calm assurance while I looked him over. He knew who he was, the perfect picture of mature, experienced, older masculinity, without any lumbago yet, and him past sixty. It had to be blindingly obvious to him that I was absolutely smitten. He was unbelievably beautiful. I sucked in the horsy man smell of him noisily, like a gasping owl, and stared at him while he posed and grinned at me.

"Caught you off guard, huh?" he said.

"I thought you were room service," I mumbled.

"I can be, if you want me to."

The next thing I knew, I was in his arms. I felt like I was home after a too long, utterly cold, lonely journey. Greedily I ran my hands through the silver wings in his hair. I'd been dying to do that since the instant I laid eyes on him. My soul had searched for this man all my life. I nestled up against him and sighed.

I heard his next words from a distance.

"What are the lines, dear? Won't you tell me about them? Whatever it is, dearest Avalon, you can tell me."

He crooned the words in my ear. Desolation swept over me. I pulled away, jerked my robe together, turned my back to him. What the hell was I thinking, forgetting how I was forced to live? I couldn't have him. The time was wrong. My quest wasn't finished and it might never be.

"Ava," he coaxed. "They are the most amazing and beautiful things I have ever seen. I can keep your secret, whatever it is."

I kept my back to him. No one had ever called me Ava. I liked it. I felt myself softening, but I held on. I had made my decision. Stubbornly, I waited for him to leave.

"Avalon, I hope you know that I am a friend to you and would never betray your secrets to anyone for any reason. I know that there are many things in this world beyond our understanding."

I held my body stiff until I hurt everywhere, both inside and out. I felt the hurt silence filling the room. Then I heard the door close. I stumbled to the bed and threw myself across it.

*

Lucian stomped down the hall to Melanie's room. She jerked the door open before he removed it from the frame with his pounding. She looked at his stormy face and stepped aside.

"Come in," she said, but he was already in the room. He stomped over to the window and stared out, his back to her. She had seen his back many times before. That's what he always did when he didn't want anyone to see his emotions. She sighed.

"I went to her room. She was wearing a robe. I saw the lines moving on her. I asked her about them. She turned me away."

He recited the information in a monotone.

"Bart says..."

Lucian turned and frowned at her. She shrugged.

"I asked him for help. He discovered through his contacts that Avalon stayed at a private island owned by a group of Shaman women. No men are allowed on the island, so it was hard for him to get information.

He couldn't find out exactly what their healing or spiritual practices are, but he says tattooing is still a spiritual practice among some indigenous groups. The tattoos can take on life and move. They are living stories. Everyone seeing them knows what that person's soul has to overcome. If the person doesn't learn what's required from their animal teachers, the lines never leave them.

If what Bart and I think is true, then Avalon is under a vow of silence about the lines on her body until they are gone, if they ever do leave, and even then, she may be under a permanent vow of silence. It's best to not mention the lines for now."

"So, the only way I can keep her in my life, is to not talk to her about the lines?"

She nodded. "I think so."

He turned on his heel and left, closing the door softly behind him. Avalon was lost to him for now, maybe forever.

A 6200 year old Indigo blue cloth holds memories of many things, including the families who kept it safe.

Çhapter 25. The Black Panther

It was time to set in motion the things I wanted to do for my family. It was time to let the past go. It had happened with Spirit's sanction and for Spirit's reasons. It was family Karma. Only Spirit knew why, but we had all been in it together from the start, and that meant something.

I contacted the solicitors taking care of Aunt Amelia's estate. They will handle my family for me. I love them and will help them, but I won't allow them to hurt me again.

*

Lucian stood in the small back room of the ancient jewelry shop studying the rare black stone he held in the palm of his hand. He moved his hand slightly, watching blue fire shoot out from its core. He nodded with satisfaction. This was her stone. A local, highly skilled silversmith would create a ring to embrace the stone. He had chosen someone from the stone's homeland to work with the gem's essence. They would know how to surround it with the calming energy of its birthplace.

He carried the stone to the silversmith himself. The silversmith immediately set to work making the silver ring. Lucian stayed on, waiting for the work to be completed. He didn't want the work rushed, and he wanted as few people as possible to handle the stone, for he trusted no one but himself to carry it safely home to its intended destination. She would need its strength.

The Black Panther

One night before I drifted off to sleep, I heard Aunt Amelia's voice again. She said, "Linen can be made into baskets, strings, nets, cords, and cloth...but people, they can transform into even greater things." Then she gave her great, hearty, purple laugh.

One starry night, when the clear, cold wind blew strong and silent across Windbay Cottage, Avalon fell into a deeper sleep than usual. In her sleep, she traveled down through inky darkness, deeper and deeper, until she became a sooty, velvet skinned black panther flowing smoothly through the night. She felt the power of her sinewy, strong muscles and the sway of her empty belly from giving birth as she walked softly on padded feet through the dark forest.

The urge in her couldn't be contained. It drove her on and on until daybreak came and she stood on the edge of a sunlit meadow. She wanted to run back to the shadows of the cool forest and hide. Panthers did not stay out in the daylight. They lived and thrived in the protective darkness.

Instead, she yearned her face forward, remembering all the stalking and feasting and birthing and living she had done. Soon she stood in the middle of the hot, sunny meadow. She glanced around. There was no place to hide her blackness, but this was where it had to happen. She would be seen, out in the open, but it couldn't be helped.

Her power left her, and she fell to the ground and slowly began to melt. Nights came and went. Rain poured over her blackness and bones while the fragrance of the meadow flowers embraced her. Scavengers came near, but left her alone, so that she remained whole in her descent.

The hot summer sun poured heat over the meadow no humans ever trod, baking the earth she lay on. She became thinner and thinner, until she melted into a speckled ointment that heated up in the sun. The ointment was flecked with gold, rich and sweet. All kinds of animals came and lapped it up. She felt herself sliding down into their bellies and she heard them give satisfied grunts of pleasure.

They each kept her for a while, then passed her through themselves, where she slid like dark, oily teardrops back into the dust or grass they walked through.

A drought came and stayed. A long time went by. The sun dried up everything around her. Everything cracked and broke apart from the heat. The roots died. The soil scattered and disintegrated. Dust blew everywhere. But she stubbornly remained in sticky, big, gold flecked, oily drops, clinging to whatever she touched in the barren meadow.

The leaves and grass and dust and animals flew by. She knew they needed her kind of help, but she didn't know what that was. Fierce heat scorched the meadow and she thinned out again. She melted far below the surface of the ground and traveled down through deep, dark places.

After a long time, she poured down into a place where sound didn't exist anymore. It was the scariest place she'd ever been. She drew in a breath. It took years. She let it out and her scream of fear rushed out into the dark silence around her, filled it, and climbed both downwards and upwards. The sound shook the soil loose around the path she had burrowed into the earth to get to where she lay.

Dark, deadly water heard her scream. It rumbled and roared beneath her and followed her sound. It filled up the space, then grabbed her up in the path it was making through the tunnel as it rushed up towards the surface of the dry, cracked earth. She wept and shouted in fear when she reached the surface, for she did not want to be born again.

The dark water diluted her. The oil she was spread out, and the more it spread and diluted, the bluer she became and the cleaner the water was. The water rushed out of the earth, and the animals suffering from the drought ran to it and drank and lived.

She felt little particles of herself sliding into them again. The rest of her was lost, and she knew it. She was not together anymore. She had been taken apart and dismembered.

She wailed and cried, causing the little spring of water the animals were drinking from to pour continually from the ground. She spread out and deepened. Finally, she quit wailing and lay flat and still for a long time.

Little grasses started rooting around her still edges. Water lilies shyly steeped themselves in her and began palely blooming. Big birds glided over her surface, dove for fish, and admired themselves in her mirrored face.

Moved only by the wind and rain and the life of the plants and animals in and around her, she no longer remembered why or how she got there. Nothing but a small memory persisted, steadily collecting itself.

Steadily, over what seemed like eons of time, the drops of black, gold flecked oil collected themselves around the memory that called out to them. One day the memory had collected all. It drew a long breath and Became again. It was painful at first. It moved muscles and hurt for a long time. It lay there, breathing and barely moving until one day, it stood up and walked slowly and painfully away from the spring of blue water.

The small black panther turned its head and yowled at the water it had separated from before it ran into the dark edges of the forest to find a hiding place.

Avalon slept on, curled under warm covers in the cold ebony night, while far away in a land of frozen green glass and impossible miracles, a silver ring set with a rare black stone rested on a bed of rich black velvet in a jeweler's shop. Surrounded by tiny, pure silver symbols, the black stone flashed blue fire steadily from its heart.

Almost any fabric pattern can be finished after starting, and sometimes is.

Chapter 26. Winter's Lee

Melanie stared out the window. Winter blew dreary icy sheets of rain in off the sea daily. Sleet and snow peppered everything, forming gray rimes on the windows. She turned away to finish preparing the tea tray for the three of them.

Lucian, Melanie and Avalon, with unspoken consent and for different reasons, chose to winter in Winter's Lee instead of traveling to milder climates.

To pass the time, they played cards or listened to music. Sometimes Lucian read to them from a rare book. Melanie liked to play old records after dinner. Sometimes Lucian asked Avalon to dance with him. They knew he asked because he wanted to hold Avalon in his arms.

Avalon had been distant to him since the outing to the cider farm, but she could never turn him down when he asked her to dance. Melanie watched the two of them exercise the greatest self-control she had ever seen in two people—except for herself and Bart, that is.

She was damn tired of waiting for Bart to make his move. Time was wasting away, and they weren't getting any younger. Would he ever pop the question? He was off on yet another six-month assignment that would keep him out of touch for most of the winter, but every few days he surfaced to call her from the only phone in the tiny village near the dig. The connection was always poor, and she had to shout to be heard. The calls were short because of the primitive connections.

Was he deliberately taking those kinds of assignments to avoid her? Surely there was other satisfying work to be done in his field; work that would enable them to be together. If he took assignments in safe countries, she could travel with him. They could go to the most interesting places in the world together. They could be companions in a fulfilling older life. They were meant to be together. She'd known it from the beginning, although it took him a little more time to realize it.

Her thoughts went back to Avalon and Lucian. Their natural flow was to be together, but they both knew they had to fight it for the time being, that there were no guarantees of a future together for them... sort of like her situation with Bart.

She picked up the tea tray and pasted a smile on her face. Today wasn't one of her better days. She had a few little twinges of pain here and there, probably from aging while she waited for Bart to finally pop the question. God only knew what all she might have wrong with her by that time!

*

The solicitors did their job. My family was taken care of with gifts and monthly stipends. Tom, Harold, Greta, Dessie, Nelson and Hanna Blue, all older than me, and still alive. I was lucky. Aunt Amelia thought so too. I giggled at the thought of her. I ticked off their names on my fingers. I'm Avalon Blue. We're a family.

I plan to turn my goodwill towards my reluctant, hostile children next. I haven't allowed them to see me the last few years, and they have stayed hurt and angered by it. I have communicated with them steadily through phone calls, letters, cards and gifts, but it hasn't been enough to keep the rift between us from widening.

First, I have to figure out how to do it. I have to go at it slow and careful. You know why.

I've been thinking about the pictures in those monthly travel magazines of unusual looking people. I'm thinking how photographs might be useful to get them used to my eccentric looks.

*

Benjamin Lawson and his son Jason were the only professional photographers in Winter's Lee. Benjamin was eighty with a proud, clipped manner of speaking. He took starkly minimalistic black and white photographs of the rugged landscapes in the area. They sold like hotcakes in the tourist shops. He never took photographs of people. His son Jason did that.

When Avalon stepped through the door, Mr. Benjamin Lawson shied away in protest. She was far too colorful for him. He barely allowed her to look at the rows of neat, black-framed pictures in his studio. He wanted her to leave, and hopefully the vision of sequins, frothy, odd colors and red hair would fade quickly from his memory. But she didn't seem to be in any hurry.

Avalon watched him. Her heart fell. This proud, haughty man was not someone she could take a risk with.

"Is there anyone else who photographs people instead of landscapes?" she asked. Benjamin felt like he had been given a sacred reprieve.

"God does answer prayers!" he murmured thankfully. "Jason!" he shouted, and hastily grabbed his coat and rushed out the front door, slamming it shut behind him.

Jason ambled in from the back room. Avalon sized up the younger Lawson. He was dressed in faded jeans, a white shirt and scruffy tennis shoes. Nothing like his father. He was tall, slim and red haired, with a cleft chin and a humorous look in his light blue eyes.

"Pardon my clothes. I've just returned from an outdoor wedding."

She stared at him and didn't speak.

"I look like my mother," he said, and grinned at her, showing large, white teeth. She waited patiently while he involuntarily circled her and appeared in front of her again.

"Would you photograph me?"

"Oookay..." he responded slowly, "but I don't need a picture. The image is forever burned in my brain."

She sucked in her breath while he looked horrified at what he had just said. Then they both laughed.

"I do admit I look somewhat unusual," Avalon said slowly, "and I am an unusual subject and there would be privacy conditions to photographing me. Legal ones."

Jason mulled over her words.

"What are the conditions?"

"First, all transactions will be under the name of Sholley Chapelin...that will be my name."

He chuckled.

"Go on."

They set appointment times when the senior Lawson would be out of the studio. She dressed in a back room in the most elaborate outfits she could devise for the sessions. She wore tunics edged with spangles, and frothy laces in rainbows of colors. She wore shoes with silver and copper adornments, nature scenes painted on them. She wore fluffy bands around her hair and small hats and large necklaces. Little animal shapes dangled from her ears and were welded onto her belt buckles.

Jason circled her each time, looking her over with camera in hand, snapping away. Beneath the orange hair and silly hats, he caught a heart shaped face, prominent gray eyes, a short nose, and a little bow mouth. Her sharp little chin jutted out as if ready for a fight.

He caught images of a lime green leotard with blue fish swimming around, a lavender tunic with small, prowling black panthers racing across it, rabbits and horses and a hawk on a red and white tunic, and mice and crows and a squirrel dancing in red and silver on a black tunic.

He laughed over an ice blue tunic with white scrolls of thin lace icebergs on it, worn over a snow-white leotard with tiny polar bears dancing around the wrists, neckline and ankles, and drew his breath in at a lilac hat with a miniature snowbird perched on it. When his eyes reached her feet, he discovered a school of tiny fish painted on her shoes. They were swimming madly in an icy blue lake surrounded by snow.

More stunning than anything was the steady way her eyes held his in the magic ransom required of him when the silver lines moved towards his hands as he arranged a stray feather or a pose. His astonishment turned to awe as he realized what he was seeing.

She left him to his own interpretation of the silver lines. His eyes met hers, and the understanding that this was beyond personal and private became solid between them. They became souls working together, young and old, devising and sharing in a cover up ritual.

At their final session, he pulled a picture from a file and handed it to her. He watched her intently as she took the picture in her hands and looked at it. She laid the picture down, then studied him with grave gray eyes.

"Why did you choose me, Sholley Chapelin?" he asked.

"You have a reputation for discretion. I'm sure you earned it by keeping secrets. This is my secret."

She walked to the window and looked out. It was a long time before she turned around.

"You see, I can't explain the lines to you, I'm not allowed to, but there is a reason for them, and they are beautiful, aren't they?"

She turned and faced him. He handed her the whole picture file.

"You are a brave woman to risk this. Your secret is safe with me, Sholley Chapelin. I didn't keep any copies of any kind. No one would believe me anyway. They would think I retouched them."

He paused, then said, "May I speak to you frankly? I have a favor to ask of you."

She nodded warily.

"I have never met or seen another woman like you, and I suspect I never will. You are a Shaman woman of some kind. I'm half your age, and half in love with you. The camera is as fascinated with you as I am. Those are some of the best pictures I've ever taken. I mean the ones without the lines showing, too. I want to photograph you and your unique clothes again."

He warmed to his subject.

"I've thought about how to do it. I could shadow your face so no one will know it's you. I know I could create award winning work with you as the subject..."

She smiled at him.

"I'm honored that you ask me. When the time comes, if it ever does, then you can take more pictures of Sholley Chapelin."

*

She chose carefully from among the pictures and sent the most colorful, overdressed ones to her children so they would get used to the way she looked now. She knew their future relationship hinged on the way she handled how she looked, her attitude, and her acting abilities.

In her letters to them, she casually mentioned the oddities she now practiced because of her "skin condition," as though it wasn't important. Over time, she threw in the information that she slept in long sleeved, high necked pajama tops and long pants, she showered privately, and wore body leotards under her clothes all the time because of her skin condition.

She told them she didn't like to be touched very much, because of her skin condition. She counted on their assuming she was just being eccentric. They did, but her daughter was unexpectedly interested in her clothes.

By the time Christmas came around, Avalon's son and daughter exchanged gifts with her through the mail. They laughed together over the phone and became more comfortable with each other. Inevitably, the time came when Michelle and Gabriel wanted her to come home.

Melanie took a picture of Avalon at the airport. She was wearing a red tunic over a purple leotard. The red tunic had tiny white ostriches rambling around on it. A long, thin, white scarf was wound around her neck and she wore red flats and carried an oversized purple purse.

Lucian held her close for a long time before he could let her go. Melanie thought Avalon looked scared and slight, forlorn and jaunty, all at the same time. She waved goodbye to them. She never said when she would return...or if she would.

Fabrics usually come with care instructions, such as use mild detergents, dry on low settings. People also come with a similar set of instructions, if you care to read between the lines.

Čhapter 27. The Traveler's Story

Lucian stomped down the beach and stopped abruptly. He stood planted in the wet sand like a large stone monolith. Heavy fog closed in around him. He ignored it. He ignored the muted sound of a foghorn blowing in the distance and the mist wetting his face, dripping down his upturned collar. He was chilled to the marrow of his bones. This damned place stayed eternally cold and dank even in the summer, and he was damn tired of it!

He was tired of Winter's Lee, the people and their short-worded, peculiar vernacular. This time he'd leave and not come back! He'd pack as soon as he got home and leave immediately for a place as far away from here as he could find.

He jerked the paper out of his pocket and read it again. He thought about throwing the paper down on the sand, but it wouldn't even make an impression. Besides, he couldn't let it go. He remembered reading the page she'd lost through the open window. That page once filled him with love and hope. This page took it all away. Bitterly he shoved it in his pocket and made his way home.

This was not the first time he'd lost a love he yearned to keep in this cold, dark place, but it would be the last, he thought grimly. This place was a jinx. He always stayed too long in Winter's Lee. That's why this happened. He should have known better. He would find another place to live. His childhood home was too full of painful memories for him to stay any longer. Why was he keeping the huge mansion his parents wouldn't even name?

*

Melanie stood in her kitchen, reading and rereading the single white sheet of paper from Avalon. It was a short, simple note, stating her intention not to return to Winter's Lee because, basically, she needed to sacrifice herself for her children.

That was how Melanie interpreted the short, plaintive note from her. She frowned at the paper. She was not surprised, for it was in Avalon's nature to sacrifice herself for others. Had Lucian received a note from Avalon too? She hurried to the phone and called him. No answer. She jerked on her coat, stuffed the note in her pocket and rushed out into the fog.

His mouth was pressed thin and tight, waves of pain emanating from him when he answered the door. He frowned and turned away from her.

"Did you get a silly note from Avalon? I did. It's a ridiculous thing. What are you doing?" she asked as her eyes swept across the luggage in the hall.

"Leaving, not that it's any of your business."

She shut the door firmly behind her and stalked past him, leading the way into the library. With another sweep of her eyes, she took in the roaring fire and the fateful missive laying on a table with a ring on it.

He crossed to a window and stood with his back to her. She sighed. She knew that old story. He didn't want her to see what he was feeling. She tapped her foot. That particular habit of his was becoming very irritating. She settled into one of the deep chairs by the fireplace to wait him out. Finally he turned from the window and settled into the chair across from her. They had been here before. In the same chairs, even.

Neither spoke. She studied his face, remembering the times they were forced to run from the hoots and blows of the other children because they were so different from them. They ran to the old cemetery at the edge of town. It became their refuge because the other children were afraid to go in.

It didn't taken them long to discover they liked running. Their muscles grew strong, and they grew agile with the delight that comes with exercise and a good childhood companion. The other children turned to new occupations when they realized Lucian and Melanie weren't afraid of them anymore.

Life had held rejections and losses for both of them. They handled them in their own ways, but when he lost Lainie and Minnie, what little humor and spontaneity he had deserted him, and moved to another country.

He fell into a deep depression. She feared for his sanity. She did everything she could to help him. She deliberately interrupted his isolation. She stayed hearty. She built up the fire, turned up the lights, chattered on about nonsense. She read the newspapers to him and commented on the financial news of the day.

Mrs. Bentley had jumped at the chance to bring them hot, fresh coffee and food, for she was terribly worried about him. She stood in the doorway wringing her hands while Melanie ate and chattered on to Lucian.

Lucian sat like a lump in a stupor, silent and stony, a dark monolith filled with insistent, bottomless grief. Months passed. She ate and chattered more. She gained weight while he remained lanky and in a dire slump of grief and self-pity.

Bloated and angry, she pictured him as a bitter old man, an ancient, lifeless, leathered relic, bent over, with a few wisps of white hair floating around his head and a forlorn look in his sunken eyes. She imagined an eon of time dragging by before he was at last ensconced on a high, tall deathbed, reaching out with a frail, bony hand, calling for Lainie and Minnie with his last breath while she sat by his deathbed, faithful, fat, white-haired, mouthy despite her ill-fitting dentures, and wrinkled. All because the damn fool wouldn't get off his ass and on with his life!

Was she up to that task again? Hell, no! Getting him to live again had been a grim, arduous task! That was decades ago, and he was still holding on to the last ragged forlorn, faded tiny, miniscule, remnants of what was left of his aged grief. With normal people, grief faded with time. It became bearable, though not forgotten. Not him!

She shook her head. Lucian owned a heart determined to see his beloveds in his own small, peculiar light. His version of faithful was forever standing in the same spot, never realizing that all people change, dead or alive, and move on.

She sighed and assessed her guilt ratio. He

HAD given her the withered roses from old Mrs. Tompkins' grave after her first boyfriend broke up with her. He HAD dragged her along the beach with one hand and shouted out baleful limericks to her when her mother passed. He HAD quoted Poe and Lovecraft to her when her father passed, and he WAS godfather to her children who loved him respectfully from a distance.

She jumped to her feet, crossed to the table, looked down at the note from Avalon and snorted.

"It's just a silly bunch of meaningless words! I'm not surprised that it threw you into yet another elongated, never ending pity party! Yes, you and Avalon are both having a pity party contest, and I will not take care of you or her through this one!"

Lucian glared at her. She glared back at him and stuck her hands on her hips.

"Think I'll stick around at least long enough to tell you a few things before you run away like she did. But first, I want you to know it's cost me plenty to go through your never ending losses with you. So you owe me. Maybe you could pay me with this ring?"

She started to touch the ring resting on top of the letter. Crafted in ornate silver, a black stone lay nestled in its center. The stone looked ancient and powerful. She felt drawn to its magnetism. She wanted to caress it, to touch it. The silver around the stone had tiny symbols carved into it. She reached for it just as he jumped to his feet and grabbed it.

She said, "Don't worry. I'm not going to say any more about you two pitiful creatures! It's time we talked about the things you've been avoiding for years."

She studied him. Anger rose again. They were old and living dreary, unfinished lives in a cove for god's sake! And at their ages, how much longer would either of them be able to remember or hear anything? She would not go through this with him again! He had to learn more about love, and not be so damned afraid of it. Love was huge and vast, touching and changing humanity through the hurts and wounds of time. Life and love were often messy and unpredictable. She had tried to tell him this before, but he always cut her off. He insisted on not being comforted. Well, this time, his sorry ass was going to listen! It was decades past time to sort out the love that lay behind their heritage.

"Listen, Lucian. People don't like Travelers, so we never pursued our heritage so we could understand who we are and what we stand for. Our two families made the choice to ignore our roots, and it kept us proud and isolated, and in an odd way, shallow with everyone, except each other.

"Have you ever wondered why your parents settled on an isolated northern seacoast instead of in a big city or on an island? Have you ever wondered why they chose to live in a little village loaded with dour fisherman who mind their own business?

"Your father made enough money to live anywhere in the world! And your beautiful mother stayed up nights and sang and played the fiddle! She wore black and red shawls and danced. Animals were soothed by her presence. She helped at the births of both people and animals. I remember the doctor calling her out to go with him. It took only her presence to make the births go easy. It was her gift to help the new come easy into this world."

She smiled in fond remembrance. He smiled back. Encouraged, she went on, "And your father! How dark and handsome he was! He could ride any horse born! There was nothing he couldn't do with leather, but he wouldn't touch it. Instead, he turned to the stones and made a fortune from them."

She glanced at him. He was listening.

"Travelers have always known about the stones, for we have had them thrown at us over and over again. We started picking them up centuries ago to try to find some value in them, to understand why people kept throwing them at us.

Your father wore black just as your mother did, and I will never know if it was in mourning for the Travelers' ways they gave up and wouldn't tell us about, or if it was in memory of them.

"Then there's my family. They were unruly and had such a hard time living on a schedule set by a ticking clock! They lived hard lives, making the exchanges needed to give up the instinctive knowledge of the beautiful, dark Mysteries endowed through our heritage so they could fit into this kind of world.

"I asked questions and got a few skimpy answers before I figured out my parents wouldn't talk about our heritage. No relatives ever came around... except KiKi LaLa... and we didn't know to ask her.

"Our families kept their vows of silence about the old ways—the Travelers' ways we sprang from. They tried to change their natural heritage. I believe that's why we are alone today, you and me. That's why we have never found our soul's solace in another. I hated being alone, so I turned to making my own roots with a man I admired and respected, but never loved with a Traveler's passion."

Abruptly, she interrupted her train of thought, "Lucian, speaking of lost love did you ever think to investigate the ship's accident? You have the resources. I like to think of Lainie and lovely little Minnie as having gotten away in one of the lifeboats, maybe living on a lost island somewhere."

She spoke harshly and recklessly, invested in startling him out of his self-pity.

"My children travel all the time. Travel is their path to reclaiming their heritage. I realized, almost too late, that they need it so they can understand themselves. Our parents are gone, and with them went the peculiar psychic fear of what our heritage is, of what the cultures we try to fit into labeled them. I'd like to tell you the Travelers' Story."

A long silence.

"Okay."

Elation ran through her. Maybe their ancestral depression wouldn't take him further down this time! She rubbed her hands together in both relief and excitement as she began the beautiful, dark, spiritual journey of their Travelers clans.

The Traveler's Story

"It is said that our four Traveler's clans have been on the road since the time of the Christ's crucifixion. Before that time, they were proud metal workers with their own guilds and knew all the secrets that metals hold.

"Our people forged irons that sang with vitality, and they made buckets that held clean air. They made silver orbs under the moon for pendants, and hammered gold frames under the sun for paintings.

"The jewelry trade looked to our clans to create the settings for the fine gemstones they sold to the rulers and other wealthy people. In those days, our small band of Travelers were proud, dark people who lived well, owned land, and were not nomads.

"Then everything changed. The rulers of that time began to use crucifixion as a punishment for crimes. Wood crosses were erected outside the city on a large hill in a barren field. The crosses were put up and taken down and used over and over again. Their wood was stained dark red with human blood.

"The rulers ordered our ancestors to make the nails for the crucifixions. Our ancestors did not want to do it, but they knew if they didn't obey, they would be put to death themselves, and they wanted to live. They also had to make the special nails that were not ordered very often. Those nails had to be extra long and the head of each one flattened into a thin circle the size of a large coin.

"Four nails for each special criminal. Those nails were designed to hold the criminal up on their cross longer so their weight would not pull their flesh through the nails and allow them to fall from the cross and die before they suffered long enough to suit their crucifiers. The cries of the crucified rang through the city streets, but our people shielded their eyes from the sight of them, and went on with their work.

"Then our ancestors heard about a man named Jesus Christ of Nazareth who had come to the city. No one dared to go see Him openly, for He spoke against the rulers of the land. Instead, our ancestors went in secret to see Him and listen to Him speak. Many of them secretly began to seek Him out after their daily work was done. They loved what He said, and believed in Him, and spread what He said to their families in secret.

"Then the rulers arrested Jesus and put Him in prison. He was tried and found guilty, and it was ordered that He be crucified. The orders came in to make a set of special nails for His crucifixion. Our ancestors knew who the nails were to be used for, and they did not want to make them, but they had to, or die themselves.

"The metal workers from each of the four main families in our clans made one nail each. They made the nails of hard metal. Then they melted silver and gold and their best precious metals and coated the nails with them. They polished the nails so they would go through the bone and flesh easier. They placed tiny pieces of the finest gemstones on the flat circles that were the nail heads. They bribed the soldiers into using those nails instead of the plain crucifixion nails.

"By that time, our ancestors had repented of ever making any crucifixion nails at all. They ran up the hill and fell at the foot of His cross and begged Him for forgiveness. But He could not give it to them. They had already chosen their Fate. The time was past for forgiveness. They would have to live with the curse for what they had done; that curse was already in place.

He heard their pleading voices and looked down on them. The beautiful gemstones on the flat nail heads sparkled through the blood flowing across them. The Christ saw the sparkle of the gemstones and knew that our four clans had honored Him with the precious gift of Beauty to help Him endure what He must.

"Because of our ancestors, there would be no painful ugliness in His memory. Instead, the power of His Beauty would always be celebrated and remembered. He knew He could not change the curse upon our people, for He saw that they were already filled with the darkness of the blood that had stained all the crucifixion nails they had ever made.

"He told them they would live, but they would be Travelers. Nomads. Wanderers. People who would never own land, or never again rest peacefully in one place for long, and they would never place a metal nail in a true home again. But since they had placed silver and gold and precious gemstones on His crucifixion nails, despite their fear of death, He would help them become the dark people they would be.

"In His compassion for the endless nights through which they would forever travel, rejected by all around them, He gave them the gift of inner sight so they might prophesy over themselves and others and know what lay ahead. He told them they would have to learn to heal themselves, for He knew they would never again be able to find doctors who could heal them.

"They listened to Him, then went sadly and sorrowfully back down the hill. The people in the city heard that the metal workers had been cursed by Him for making crucifixion nails, and they turned them out of their homes and drove them away from the city.

"The metal workers and their families went on the road. They tried to find new places to live, but the curse always traveled ahead of them and they were turned away every place they went.

"Centuries passed. Nobody knew quite when our families became known as Travelers. They roamed Europe and developed their own languages, songs, and habits. They learned to build small houses on wagons, using wood pegs for nails, so they could carry their homes with them. They wore their own kind of clothes and put touches of red on them as a reminder of their ancestors mistake.

"The Earth became Hallowed to them, and they learned its rhythms. They made their own dances to match the Earth's rhythms, for they had no church to go to and no leader. Over time, they were glad they didn't.

"Musical and handsome, they used their gift of foretelling to sing and play the fiddle and tambourine and tell fortunes to make a living in the towns they passed through. They learned about horses, for they had to have them. They learned the art of smudging to cleanse one's self, for often they were not near water and it was not their favorite element anymore. They had become fire and earth people.

"Nature taught them, for they could not stay in earth homes. They developed their healing skills with animals, plants, and through understanding nature. They made their own salves, herbal compounds, and incantations.

"They did not keep albums or diaries because they had to keep moving and travel light. Instead, they illustrated their bodies with symbols, lines, stories, and tattoos, to pass their stories and values down to the children gathered around the campfires.

"As it is with all people, some of the Travelers tried to put their roots down in a place outside their heritage, which was what our parents did. They tried to change into something they were not. Many of them became ashamed of being Travelers because rooted people look down on all nomads and always have.

"Because of this silly shame, our people stopped telling their future generations about the Travelers' heritage that lives on in their souls. They wanted their new generations to fit in with the rooted people, causing great opposition in their souls.

"The new generations of Travelers felt the ancient curse that had been handed down to them, but the spiritual nature of it was never explained. They didn't know they were naturally nomadic, that the ways of the wind was seeded in them through their spiritual nature. So they moved away from the old ways.

"Psychic, sad, and passionate, they bought houses and stopped traveling. They sought an understanding not possible in the new world they lived in without knowing the history of what and where they sprang from. Their children's own fierce, independent, passionate souls, inclined to natural darkness, the magnetic force essence, eventually became a mystery to themselves, a curse to fight and overcome. They came to fear themselves just as the rooted people feared them.

"People who aren't Travelers don't understand the intensely magnetic Nature that causes us to have a deeper understanding and a natural spiritual alignment with the Darkness. We understand that natural Darkness is just as Holy as natural Light. We understand this with our soul.

"These days, Traveler's children go to doctors and therapists for treatment and for drugs because doctors and therapists have convinced them that they are depressed, or in some level of dysfunction. They try to live like the fixed society they were dropped into, to live by their values, but it can't work unless someone comes along and tells them the truth of what it means to be descended from the Travelers. Only then can their spirits begin to understand the journey they are taking and make a choice about moving on or staying.

"There are very few of the older generations of our Travelers left. Many of them don't remember the old stories any more. The new generations are aimless wanderers."

Her words stopped. She was emptied out. Silence filled the room. A log sparked and resettled in the fireplace.

Lucian stirred and asked, "Why didn't you tell me this before?"

"You wouldn't have heard me," Melanie replied. "You didn't want to know. In a way, I don't blame you. Knowing our history is like walking a tightrope."

Melanie continued, "The Travelers' tattoos were moving, living lines on our ancestors. They had to become artful dodgers, just like Avalon. It is no accident that Avalon came into our lives. She's as lost as we ever were, but she has no good, strong, dark heritage to cling to, like we do. Pity her for that. We have our heritage, our psychic abilities and our roots here, but I believe Avalon went to that island without any of that backup, and her initiations have left her homeless.

"I think she has always been homeless in some ways, so it came down to understanding her soul's journey so she can live. The lines forced her to become a Traveler, like us. The moving lines on her, whatever they are, speak the language of her soul. The lines are a map for her journey and they make her one of us, so we cannot abandon her. I think that a part of her journey is done, for she has found her children again. Those are roots she can cling to, that she understands. Don't try to take that away from her, Lucian, by wishing her back here."

"You mean like I did with Lainie."

It was a statement, not a question.

She sighed and said, "Yes. Every Traveler's journey takes them to places that have something they need, at least for a while. And no one can predict how long that need will last. It cannot be planned like a business trip. It will take as long as it must, and you must stay here and wait and go on loving Avalon as though she were right here."

Tears sprang to the surface and she managed to say, "Just as I am doing with Bart."

Startled at her own unexpected, painful confession, she jumped to her feet. "Can I have the ring?" she gestured hopefully at the gorgeous ring resting in his hand.

"No!"

She smiled and slid into her coat.

"No harm in trying."

Moss has many uses, one of which is to soften the clothing of elves.

Chapter 28. The Buffalo Mother

This is the story of the Buffalo Mother.

Far away in a prairie kingdom lived a pretty maiden. Her hair was pale green and wavy and trailed far behind her, erasing all the footprints she had ever left on Earth.

The maiden walked endlessly, weeping silent, golden tears. They fell to the right and left of her as she traveled ceaselessly across the hot, barren prairie. Sometimes the maiden came to high hills and climbed them and stood on top. She held her hands above her eyes to shade them from the sun and stared out across the empty prairie. There was never anything to see, only short, waving grass in a few places and dusty brown ground everywhere else.

Then one day, a Buffalo appeared on the horizon. The pretty maiden was sitting down on flat ground, wiping her tired feet with her long green hair when she saw the Buffalo standing on a great hill far away in the distance.

The Buffalo stomped its feet and spoke to her through the vast silence stretching across the distance between them. The maiden listened to the voice of the Buffalo speaking. The Buffalo said its heart was in great pain, for it had lost the herd it belonged to and its children and could not find them again.

Then the maiden heard the Buffalo wheeze, and the ground shook. She heard a great thud as it hit the ground. The sound rang across the prairie in great circles from where the Buffalo had been standing. Dust flew up between the maiden and the setting sun. The Earth shook where she sat. She fell over and grabbed the skinny, short grasses around her and held onto them. When she looked up again, she couldn't see the Buffalo anymore.

The maiden got down on all fours and crawled across the prairie toward the hill where the Buffalo once stood. She crawled on and on, day after day. She stopped only to sleep and eat the grains the grass dropped, and to drink the brine from the golden tears of sorrow she constantly shed.

Summer passed and the maiden kept moving on. She rested her heart on the ground, laying out full length on the Earth when she stopped at night. She felt the heat and the blood of the Earth's rhythm rocking her as she curled into a ball and covered herself with her long green hair.

Fall set in and the grasses became brown and brittle. Bitter seeds fell from them and the maiden ate them and spit out the chaff. Her endless tears caused brown salt cracks in her face that leaked ceaselessly. The water from them made hard, spatting noises when they fell on the dark, cracked ground. She lapped up the tears and tasted their bitterness and stood it, for there was no other water to be had. And still she crawled on.

One day, she reached the bottom of the hill the Buffalo once stood on. She looked up and measured the high hill with her eyes. Then she curled into a ball, pulled her hair over herself and rested.

When she woke, snowflakes were falling. Her long green hair had grown longer while she slept, and it was covered with snowflakes. She began to crawl up the slope of the hill, her long green hair flowing behind her, making curves in the snow, leaving a trail for whoever came after her to follow. When she reached the top of the hill, she saw the Buffalo's heart laying on the ground, steaming fresh and hot, cradled within the Buffalo's sun bleached white bones.

She was hungry. She crawled over to it and licked it with her tongue, then cradled herself inside the Buffalo skeleton and began to eat the heart. Throughout the long winter, the maiden ate of the Buffalo's heart. It nourished her and kept her from starving.

The snow fell and the wind swept across the prairie month after month, banking the snow into the few places it could find. The top of the hill stayed bare and alone, except for the wind, which allowed only a little bit of snow to tarry there.

The woman curled her long, green hair around herself and the steaming, warm Buffalo heart each night and listened to the Buffalo heart's steady beat as she lay there. The winter seemed never-ending to her.

One day, her tears dried up and she knew the time would come when there would be no more Buffalo heart to eat. Just then, a crow landed beside her and swaggered around. The woman curled her hair over what was left of the Buffalo heart to hide it from the crow.

The crow cocked its head and looked at her before it flew off the side of the hill. The woman sat up and looked around. She uncovered the heart and saw that only a little bit was left. She looked at the pale green hair around herself and felt of the wrinkles on her face. She was cold. She touched her teeth with her tongue and felt their needle sharpness. They were fangs now. She tried to stand up but could not. She had to stay on both her hands and feet. She looked down at her hands and feet and saw that they had become paws.

Ah! She was an animal now. Maybe tomorrow, she would discover what kind of animal she had turned into. She curled back around the little bit of heart that was left, ate the rest of it and went to sleep again.

The snow came down and covered her up and the pretty maiden's spirit left to be with the Buffalo mother's spirit. Together, they hunted ceaselessly across the empty prairie for their homes and their herds and their lost children. This is the Way of women.

It Is Never the End

Avalon laid the pen down and closed the diary. She stared out the window at the dripping, bare branches of the trees in the yard. She could see the tiny, rough edges all along their branches. Spring buds would soon burst out of them.

She laid her head down on her arms on the writing desk and cried while the Buffalo Mother and its companion softly and wearily made their way over the edge of the world and out of sight.

Leftover fabrics cause verbal creativity to spring forth, especially at eventide and when attending quilting bees.

Ćhapter 29.   Reclaiming a Lost Heritage

Lucian surveyed the confused jumble in the attic. It was past thirty years since anyone had been up here. He never came up here. Not since he carried the last of Lainie's and Minnie's things up.

He was up here now because of the Travelers' story. His heart had been opened by it; it was high time to unravel the mystery instead of trying to avoid it or hold it too close. Mourners tend to dwell in the shadows. It was time for him to give that up, too.

He looked around. The cavernous space was divided into two huge rooms taking up the entire third floor of the house. Old boxes were carelessly piled into unorganized heaps. Furniture, mirrors, paintings, and other things stood or leaned here or there. Everything was layered with cobwebs and dust as thick as the finger he ran across a dresser top.

The lighting was skimpy and primitive. There was one small bulb hanging from the ceiling on a long cord in each room. He looked up at the tiny, unfinished windows high above him. He shook his head. His parents, who spared no expense in building this huge, elegant house, left the attic unfinished. Why? Maybe they thought of an attic as a storeroom. Certainly they discouraged his ever playing in it. When a child, he was curious about the attic, but as he grew up, he forgot about it.

He took a deep breath. It was time to do this, starting today. What he learned didn't matter anymore. For the first time, he no longer feared knowing.

The Travelers' Story had changed him. He would no longer obey his parents' unspoken commandments to never know, to never go too near life or the attic.

He planned to handle everything in stages. He would be the only one touching the things up here.

Each day he climbed the stairs and cleared and cleaned and stacked and learned. He cleared a space and moved his old rocking horse and other childhood toys into it.

After everything important and private to him was hid from prying eyes, he called in a cleaning crew, electricians and carpenters. They went to work. Weeks of noisy hammering, measuring and construction sped by. When the work was finished and everyone gone, he began opening boxes.

He soon filled the new shelves in the attic with fine sets of dishes, stacks of smooth linens and wonderful books, things his parents had collected on their travels. Now and then he stopped to set aside a small wood crate with a label bearing a strange language printed on it.

He worked steadily until the day came when all that remained to open were the few small crates he'd set aside. He ran a hand over the top of one, wondering what was in it. But instinctively, he knew it wasn't time to open it. He looked around. Something still needed to be done.

He studied the storage shelves. The attic was filled with his parents and Lainie's and Minnie's things. But he didn't want the attic to be a coffin filled with newly organized bunches of nostalgic remains! He wanted to leave feeling better than when he entered. No getting swamped with pity and nostalgia for anything in the past again. He needed this place just for himself. No outside influences in here, dead or alive. No more.

He studied the small stack of crates. He needed to be alone with them when he opened them. An idea came to him. Why not convert a few of the large bedrooms on the second floor into storage and display rooms for their things? The china could go down to the kitchens and dining rooms, the rugs into the great rooms. He would find places for the rest of their things. They would no longer be hidden in the attic, but admired and appreciated throughout his house.

A new wave of work began. When the second-floor rooms and other places in the house were ready, the attic room treasures were moved under Mrs. Bentley's supervision.

As soon as everything was out, a new lock was installed and he pocketed the only key.

Mrs. Bentley left early at his urging. He locked the door behind her and climbed the attic stairs two at a time.

He turned on the lights then locked the door behind him. At last, he was alone. The memories of Lainie, Minnie, and his parents were honored. Mrs. Bentley discreetly removed many things to the basement storerooms until the time came when they would no longer be painful reminders, just gentle reminders of past loves he could ponder.

The small bunch of unopened crates stacked in a corner was all that remained. He looked at the crates appraisingly. Instinctively, he knew opening them would lead him into his new future, into a new beginning. Something old was at last ready to let go. Something new was ready to begin.

He went to the stack of crates and knelt beside them. He picked up the small hammer he placed there earlier. He chose a random crate, pulled it to him, and applied the hammer to its top. The nails came out of the ancient wood slats with complaining, screeching noises, as though they were protesting giving up their long-held secrets.

He set the top aside. The scent of wood smoke on dark nights wafted out of the crate. He sniffed. A strange joy stirred his blood. He reached in the crate. His fingers touched smooth, cool silk. Gently he lifted out an ancient black dress. He stood up and held the dress out in front of him. It unfolded slowly, whispering down to ankle length. The dress was handmade in a simple peasant style, with a full skirt, a round neckline and short sleeves. Tiny rows of embroidered red flowers edged the bottom of the skirt. This was a dress for a celebration. He studied it with narrowed black eyes, not knowing that a very long time ago, someone else with the same kind of black eyes had studied it too.

He turned the dress this way and that, listening to the silky whisper. He noticed hundreds of what looked like pinholes in the dress but couldn't figure out what they were. A tall, weighty woman would have worn this dress.

On impulse, he held the smooth silk to his face and drew in the smell of it, imagining what the woman would have looked like. An unfamiliar loneliness swept through him. Suddenly, he heard the call of the wind outside the large new windows. The sound stirred the very cells of his being. He felt an intense urge to fling open the windows, to travel with the wind, to find an open road. He stood alone in the silent attic with the rooted world outside sedately and mannerly passing by, and he was at last completely glad he wasn't out there in it, being understood and accepted.

He felt his Traveler's individuality resurrecting itself. He felt the scattering of the roots and remnants that stood in the way of it, loosing and flying away with the wind.

His head drooped forward. He sighed. He was so very tired of something, but he didn't know what. He rested his cheek against the old black dress and began to imagine he was young again, that an old, dark, merry grandmother was holding him. He remembered the Travelers story. He imagined the creak of wagon wheels forever moving on. He imagined himself with Travelers. Their voices surrounded him with a new, strange, comforting language he'd never heard before. It was a language his soul recognized and called its own.

He sank to the floor beside the crate, cradling the black dress in his arms. Old loves and living ways that were never been lost, only forgotten for just a little while, flooded his soul with their ancient heritage. Slowly he returned to the home that always lived deep within him. Exultation filled his being. He realized the purpose behind the work done in this space.

He was preparing this place, this attic, for this lost part of himself. He was making a home for his lost heart. A heart wasn't a simple thing. It was a human place holding many things and ways, among them, different kinds of courage and loves and hates, and yes, hats.

As he lay there, his heart expanded and soared. He finally understood that Lainie would always love him, as he would always love her and Minnie. It was a natural and good love, despite their differences. And, their differences once merged long enough to bring beautiful Minnie into the world.

He stretched out on the floor and looked up, searching for Spirit in one of its many names, as every soul does when it reaches a crossroads. The old hurts melted from around his heart as the attic expanded and opened out into space. He watched vines climb the smoky, wood scented attic walls and mysterious, pale flowers bloom from them.

This was his sanctuary. A place he never knew was waiting for him, a place where the soul of his people dwelt. He finally came home to this attic room roosting high above dark water dashing itself and mourning against black cliffs. They'd waited here until he was ready to accept the Travelers' way of being his parents withheld from him.

He suddenly realized that knowing his true heritage before they passed would have separated him from his beloved parents too soon. But they were gone now. So were Lainie and Minnie.

It was time to shed his habit of avoidance, to stop living as a self imposed outcast. His lost family was with him. Now he could go forward.

Melanie was right. He was no longer a child or even a young man. He once assumed that having one friend who knew him so well would be enough to last a lifetime. But it wasn't enough anymore, like it was when they were young. It was time for him to start looking for others to understand him and for others who needed to be understood by him.

Maybe it was the loss of Avalon, along with the Traveler's story that woke him up to seeing his half-life. Whatever the reason was, he was grateful.

He thought of the agency investigating Lainie's and Minnie's deaths. He assumed the investigation would be fruitless, but it was one he needed resolved before he could divest himself of his last remnants of grief over them and move on.

He was well aware of how his peculiarities separated him from the rest of the world. He used to be proud of them. His wealth and the isolation of Winter's Lee had neatly insulated him. He'd grown up with doting parents in a huge house with maids and cooks. There was a nanny when he was small. And he had never asked any questions, or gone near the attic.

He was given most everything his heart desired, and when something he really wanted came along, he patiently set out to have it without ever questioning why he wanted it. He had learned well from his parents.

Melanie was the only person who understood his peculiar intensity. She was a lifelong friend, a companion Traveler to his soul.

After a while he sat up, laid the black dress aside and reached into the crate again. He lifted out fringed shawls and scarves and stacked them beside the black dress. In the bottom of the crate he found a pair of wide, black leather women's shoes. He held them up and examined the worn soles of the heavy shoes, wondering how many miles they trod. He placed them back in the crate, laid the other things on top of them, and fastened the lid in place.

He pried the lid off the second crate and discovered a small boy's faded cap perched on top. He picked up the jaunty little cap and instantly knew it was his father's. The cap was black satin and silk with a crimson red lining. Beneath it lay a child's tambourine, a tin plate, cup and silverware. The rest of the box held a small girl's dress made of red and black silk and a boy's black suit with a red silk handkerchief tucked into the pocket.

He remembered his mother sedately playing classical violin when company came. After they left, she turned the violin into a fiddle and danced on the cliff top while his father laughed and capered about.

Suddenly he was exhausted. The past months had been hectic with the chase towards a new understanding, a new way of living. He wanted it, needed it, yes, but he could go no further without rest. He accepted it and lay down, pillowing his head on the children's clothes his parents had worn. The combined scents of horses and campfires lulled him to sleep.

*

He moved the crates to his rooms. During the next weeks, he discreetly consulted with experts about preserving the Travelers' things in the crates. What he did was nobody's business. Anyway, Melanie was gone with Bart on some godforsaken dig.

Experts on furniture and preservation and an architect came and went. The carpenters, handymen, window installers and others were busy with new work.

*

On a late fall day, Lucian stood in the attic surveying the finished attic. The summer had passed in a flurry of work. Fall was almost gone. The cavernous attic rooms were now planked in pale, varnished wood to allow as much light as possible. The high ceilings and long walls were insulated and covered with the same pale, luminous wood. Tall glass showcases with cunning latches and well-placed interior lights rimmed the long walls. In them stood mannequins dressed in the Travelers' clothes from the crates.

Huge windows in all four walls replaced the high, tiny windows. The new windows let in a flood of natural light, giving a spectacular view of the cliffs and sea below. He gave a final look around, locked the door behind him and pocketed the key. It was time to leave. His luggage sat in a neat row in the hall.

*

Winter came while Lucian worked and traveled and sought out more of his branch of the Travelers clans. He scoured Europe to find his people and to find out what he could about his parents' backgrounds. He discovered stories of passion, hate and love and death, and they caused his heart and soul to ache and steadily expand into more understanding and love.

When he discovered his mother's lineage still used animal tattoos to gain spiritual understandings, relief and hope overtook him and at last became his companions.

Avalon! Without her sacred, well kept secret, there was no possibility of a relationship between them. He came to the understanding of it later than her. Melanie and Avalon had led the way, revealing something beyond the mundane, awakening him to the path he was now following.

He accepted his loss, and after a while, it began to seem like a long time ago that he secretly wept over losing Ava—his Avalon. He knew now that his love for her would always be a part of him, for without the silly, funny ways of the muddy, wailing, accidental little messenger flung into his arms, he would have lost his life to his misery. She and Melanie had saved his soul.

But he still harbored tender memories made of guts and reckonings, sweet purple dancing and prancing forth past war zones. That hope was born when a scrap of paper flew out an open window on a rainy night and fell into his hands. And oh, how he longed to someday find Avalon again and protect her from too much of the world, and put a permanent stop to their aloneness.

Umbrellas made of taffeta with fringed silk edges are nice, particularly pink ones, but sensible canvas raincoats with button up hoods keep you drier.

Chapter 30. The Little Sea Otter and the White Swan

Avalon stared out the dining room window, absently rubbing a pink painted fingernail along the edge of the new colorful business cards. She should be having fun. She was now the co-owner of an exciting boutique selling body leotards and tunics exclusively designed by her. Her enthusiastic daughter designed and made jewelry with animal themes to complement the leotards and tunics. They were making a lot of money and Michelle was joyfully expanding their business.

Gabriel, her earnest accountant son, dryly thanked her for her gift of money and immediately invested it in his children's educations. Now they would not have to work to get through school, furthermore, they could choose the school they attended.

She grinned to herself. Because of the money, the grandchildren thought of her as just eccentric, not the crazy, weird or mean grandmother they always heard about, the one who forever did their parents dirty. They were busy running around spending money and having fun doing it. That was fine with her. It would go on for a little while, but not for too long.

For now, they accepted her foibles and her weird privacy needs without question. She learned that everyone has Shadows. She saw it in her children and remembered it in her family. Everywhere she looked, there they were. Maybe they were the glue that held genetics together.

She should be happy and satisfied, and mostly she was, but secretly, she wished that Lucian and Melanie would have tried to find her. She sent them notes saying she wasn't coming back. That didn't work. Evidently they'd believed her and got on with their lives. That was months ago. Didn't they miss her? Her mouth trembled and curved down in misery. Work. It was all that was left to her. Work would have to do for the rest of her life.

*

That night a little Sea Otter visited her dreams. It was a pleasant visit. The little Sea Otter showed up again the next night. Then it started showing up every night. It always arrived when she was just on the verge of falling asleep.

It came to get her to pay attention. It floated on its back, groomed itself, and broke open clamshells. It wanted her to know something, and it chattered and splashed and swam around, but it couldn't get her to understand.

In her dreams, she began swimming with the little Sea Otter; she swam alongside it, listened to its chatter, and felt a new flexibility growing in her body as she curved and dove through the water beside it.

She felt the simple, joyful influence of the Sea Otter lingering throughout the day. She began walking, gaining a new kind of happy strength. She took up going to the ballet and eating popcorn in the park. Then she made friends with a few of the women in the park. She exchanged greetings with the people in her neighborhood.

But that wasn't enough for the little Sea Otter. It wanted her to dive deeper. She didn't want to, she was content. She wouldn't budge, so the little Sea Otter started sending catastrophic dreams night after night while it lay on its back watching her, munching delicacies.

In dream after dream, she lost everything. Lucian, Melanie, Aunt Amelia, her children. She kept losing, losing, losing. She couldn't stand it anymore. She ordered the little Sea Otter to go away. She told it she didn't have the kind of courage it wanted her to have; that she couldn't stand steady for people through life and death and illnesses. She wasn't reliable. Nobody should rely on her. Not all the names for GOD that existed could change that fact! She only knew how to run away. That was all there was to it. She insisted and argued, "You can't change what is!"

Finally she shouted, "Go away!"

The little Sea Otter dove into the water and swam away. She cried as she watched it leave. It didn't come back. For a few nights, she didn't dream at all.

The White Swan

Aunt Amelia spoke to her again one night just as she was falling asleep.

"Feathers and mohair both provide certain kinds of fantastic flight." Aunt Amelia's big purple laugh faded away as Avalon found herself standing under a leafy green tree on the banks of the stream where she always met the little Sea Otter. A motion caught her eyes. She looked out over the water at the far away bend in the stream. She watched as side by side, the little Sea Otter and a tall, stately, White Swan swam toward her.

The little Sea Otter swam near and began chattering. She finally understood its words. It asked the White Swan for help because she was dense, very dense, in the little Sea Otter's opinion, and it didn't have time to waste; there was playing and eating to be done, there was touching and grooming and companionship waiting.

She looked at the White Swan. It was filled with dignity and grace. Avalon could tell the White Swan loved the little Sea Otter. The White Swan swam towards her and stopped a few feet away. It turned its head and looked at her. She sucked in her breath. The White Swan didn't have any eyes. The sockets where they should have been were empty and full of Light. Shock ran through her, followed by a great sadness for the beautiful White Swan. A tremendous yearning filled her. Impulsively, she waded into the water and dove in. She came up underneath the White Swan and stood up in the water. The White Swan's empty body settled over her. She grew wings and a beak and her eyes filled with Light. She groomed herself and settled into the water and began swimming in stately circles.

Her swan's heart reached out to the little Sea Otter swimming around her and they touched hearts. The Swan she had become loved the little creature completely, and the sweetness of it shattered the defenses around the human heart of the dreamer into a thousand pieces.

The pieces fell from the Swan and lay floating on the surface of the lake. The Swan

swam in ever widening circles. The broken
pieces bobbed away to other places in the
ripples. The soul of the beautiful White Swan
swam ever deeper, carrying the heart of the
sleeping dreamer into new places of grace and
forgiveness.

*

Avalon circled herself for the next few days,
observing the new things she was doing, and
coming to terms with them. Everyone made
mistakes and had limitations, but they went
ahead and enjoyed life. So why shouldn't she?

Actually, why shouldn't she keep the living
tattoos? There were a few of them left. It was
her business if she did. Not anybody else's.
She'd gone through hell to get them. They were
awesome, spiritual, and rejuvenating. And they
were her friends. She had learned to pet them
correctly, and now used the organic, bio-
degradable products they preferred. She wore
lightweight, all cotton blends to sleep in. There
was much more. She once asked for overtime,
but she knew better now.

She was finally making friends, and she
didn't want to give them up. Maybe she didn't
want to learn more spiritual hoo hah, and
watch those friends vanish, too. Maybe she
would have both, friends and trifling,
complaining, moving lines she was forced to

pet. Maybe she would be just what she already was with both of them! Whatever that was. Surely there was a way to do it.

She thought about the tattoo parlor she passed on her way to the park, lingering sometimes to watch the owners and their clients. There were four tattoo artists. Two young girls and a guy, and Tolliver, an old man with white hair. All the tattoo artists dressed in gothic black, wore long hair, and were covered in tattoos. They used loud voices, cussed, and were surly with most people. They bore the hearty daring of Earth warriors, the delicate touch and skills of surgeons, and an eye for strange beauty, along with a tendency to ride motorcycles someplace every night and become inebriated.

Well, she mused, she owned photographs of herself with the lines moving in them, and she managed that well with Jason Lawson. He was a loyal friend by the time they were done with the photography.

Was Tolliver the tattoo artist someone she could trust, too? The strong urge she'd been resisting for a very long time overcame her. She grabbed her purse and headed out the door. She would begin it now, while she still had the courage. It helped that the lines loved the tattoo parlor and wanted more, too.

*

Avalon left the tattoo parlor at midnight. She looked down with satisfaction at the small White Swan swimming on the instep of her left foot. It was beautiful! And, it companioned the little Sea Otter swimming on the instep of her right foot.

She'd finally trusted Tolliver enough, with encouragement from the living lines that went into withdrawal whenever she hesitated. At night he tattooed small sea waves on her cheekbones, while the lines reached up to touch the warmth of his hands. The lines settled for rocking in the tiny waves and waterfalls and spirals tattooed on Avalon's cheekbones, neck and face. They stayed still long enough for Tolliver to draw their animal faces, paws, and outlines on Avalon's arms and shoulders and hands. He tattooed a full moon on her nape, an eagle on her shoulder, and a ground hog and mole on her belly.

He quit drinking by the time he completed their secret, middle of the night tattooing sessions. He packed his bags and Avalon paid his way to an art school in France and sent his motorcycle with him.

Avalon edged cautiously out into daylight, searching for more companionship. Once people got past her eccentric looks, they accepted her. The lines moved openly as her emotions changed, but people didn't notice, for they traveled in the tattoo paths Tolliver had inked for them. People thought the lines were somehow part of the tattoos. When they did notice, Avalon was perfecting ways of covering for the lines.

Most people didn't mind the older woman with the animal tattoos all over her short, ample body, her orange hair and strange clothes, for her smile was radiant upon them and her step was benevolent.

Tinsel and fat quarters for quilting, felt for homemade projects. But what about cashmere from goats, and vicuna from a llama-like animal with orange fur and white patches for more lordly endeavors?

Chapter 31. The Stubborn Little Donkey

Avalon was remembering the diary page she lost in the rain so long ago. Christmas was coming soon. Sure, she appreciated her children, but she missed Melanie and Lucian.

She sighed. That time was gone forever. They were, no doubt, traveling the world with matching luggage, tall, sophisticated and perfectly mannered in impeccable, perfectly tailored black clothing.

She was short and eccentric. *"Let's face it. I never fit in with them."* she thought to herself. She ran a tattooed hand over the tiny dark blue dragonflies drifting across her sky blue tunic. Blue morning glories edged her midnight blue leotard at ankles, wrists, and neck. She raised her eyes to the window, not seeing the snow or any of the world outside.

She sat frozen in a twilight world of loneliness, listening to the clock ticking time away until a stubborn little donkey clopped its way across her mind.

Surprised at the noisy interruption, she watched as the little donkey ambled through her mind, clopping along cutely and loudly. She laughed with delight at the sound the little donkey made with its hooves. *Who wouldn't laugh?* she thought. Instantly, she forgot her misery.

Was this the little Christmas donkey? She chuckled. The little Christmas donkey had carried bags and boxes and Joseph and Mary and Jesus. They sat on the donkey's strong little back while it carried them just where they needed to go. That same little donkey had followed their wishes instead of its own. That same little stubborn donkey had carried the Christ, providing transportation to a place for them to stay so they could begin a history that changed the world.

Maybe she needed to begin a history that changed her world. She laughed at herself. She was sort of like a donkey. Not the Christmas donkey, of course, just one of the many stubborn ones carrying their burdens, and having to do their part.

But wasn't there something holy in everything? Sometimes people's burdens were lighter and sometimes heavier, and who was to say for how long they should be toted around? Maybe the end was in sight, and wasn't Christmas just the time to make such a shift?

Maybe if she turned a corner real quick, her burdens might slide off and get lost; tumble right over a ridge or dune or something clear out of sight, never to be seen again. She could spray a lemon scented deodorizer in the direction they disappeared so they wouldn't stink, just remain an unsolved Mystery.

The stubborn little donkey smiled at her with large brown eyes and hee-hawed in a loud voice, as if it understood everything she was thinking.

She jumped up, pulled on her coat and grabbed her purse. There was something she needed to do, and she had put it off long enough because of her silly stubbornness!

*

The snow was still falling when she stepped out of the jewelry store carrying a bag with two small white boxes in it. In each box lay half of an ancient, used silver heart. Each heart was designed to break into two pieces so it could be shared with a significant other. Each half had a fine silver chain attached to it. She stopped in the street and opened the boxes and admired the silver hearts. She touched the two half hearts hanging around her neck to let a little of the snow and her hopes into them.

Cotton and terry make fine dishcloths and tablecloths. But what about a cookie jar? Doesn't it deserve a fashionable cover?

Chapter 32. Cookies and Chocolate Cakes

Melanie was baking Christmas cookies and thinking about Bart. All the children were coming home for Christmas. It was true, they all liked Bart, at least the few times they'd seen him! She slapped the wood spoon into the bowl of melted butter.

His dry language and absentmindedness reminded them of their beloved old professor father and grandfather. The grandchildren crawled all over him while he told stories about the digs he investigated.

She stopped stirring and frowned. God, he was slow! Years had passed! How much time did he think was left for either of them? They were both more than sixty years old! She had a sudden vision of dying a lingering death at two hundred- eighty-seven years, sixteen days, and three hours old, after waiting for him to propose; he finally tossed a ring into the casket at her funeral and mumbled a belated, apologetic proposal over her corpse.

Bart seemed to have some of Lucian's reluctance to face up to what was needed. Were they related in some strange way? Other than both being extremely stubborn men? If she didn't have a ring on her finger soon, she would have to have him hypnotized, or dose him with something! Maybe a potion?

*

The past few months have certainly been insightful, Bart muttered ruefully to himself, what with Melanie snapping at him every minute. He knew what was needed, but a sense of impending doom kept nagging at him and stopping him, causing him to put it off almost too long. He snapped the lock on his suitcase shut, picked up the heavy ring box from the bedside table and stuffed it into his pocket. It was time to leave for the airport.

Time passed slowly while he made snow forts, threw snowballs, told stories, and held learned discussions with the adult children while waiting for a chance to be alone with Melanie.

Now that he finally decided to do the deed, he was extremely anxious to get on with it. In vain, he followed Melanie around, waiting desperately for any opportunity to be alone with her before Christmas was over and gone, with just a dull memory left behind.

At last the opportunity came! The house was empty for a few hours. All the diabolical, cursed children were in the village, doing even more Christmas shopping. Even the crying babies were gone, he didn't care where! His heart filled with an unholy glee as he secretly wished them all to be gone until the Fifth of Never! They were the clever ones!

He knew he didn't have much time, for they would somehow figure out that he wanted them gone. Perverse as they were, they would rush back and take her away from him again! He needed to make it quick, come to the point and all that. All the things that he was not good at, not good at all.

He discovered her in the kitchen mixing chocolate frosting. He strolled into the kitchen, humming like he didn't have a care in the world. She looked up from the frosting and paused, then observed, "I don't think I've ever heard you hum before."

He stopped rumbling immediately. She studied him a minute while he looked innocently back at her. Then she pulled her eyes away and went back to mixing chocolate frosting. He fingered the velvet ring box in his pocket as he edged closer and closer to her. He opened his mouth to speak to her, and suddenly couldn't breathe. He found himself standing over her, gaping like a landed fish. He could imagine what he looked like, looming over her with his mouth open, and it wasn't good. She looked up at him.

"Oh, you want a bite?"

She broke a piece off a sugar cookie from a nearby plate and placed it in his open mouth. He closed his mouth and obediently chewed. A long, silent minute went by. Then she handed him the mixing spoon.

"Taste the frosting and see if it's okay."

He stared at the spoon. It was coated with a thin layer of chocolate frosting. Then he stared at her face. She'd already tasted the frosting. He knew because a smudge of it was by her mouth.

He stared at her while he licked the frosting off the spoon. Finally she took the spoon away from him and said something, he didn't know what. Then she went to wiping the counter with a dish towel.

He couldn't stand it anymore. He had to do it right now. His nerves would get the best of him if he waited, and he would run as fast and as far away as he could! He would never have the guts to come back, so it was now or never! He grabbed her arm, whirled her around, plucked the dish towel from her hand, tossed it across the room, then grabbed her face in his hands and licked the smudge of chocolate frosting off the side of her mouth with his tongue.

He sighed and drew back and looked at her. He couldn't stand the look in her eyes. It made him want to do all kinds of things, crying being just one of them. He slammed her tight to his chest so she couldn't stare at him. He closed his eyes and smoothed her hair back madly for a minute. Then the words burst out.

"Melanie, you simply must marry me."

At the end of his words, his panic caught up with him. He clutched her convulsively as his breath started coming and going in big gulps. From a distance he recognized the signs of a full-blown panic attack coming on. He rolled his eyes around the kitchen to avoid making eye contact with her. He knew that if he looked at her, somehow he would be doomed and lost forever.

She pulled out of his arms, grabbed a small brown bag out of a drawer, opened it and blew into it. It formed a sort of paper balloon.

"Here. Breathe into this!"

She tried to hand it to him. He grabbed it, and the ring box clutched in his numb fingers tumbled to the floor. He tottered over to a chair and fell heavily into it. The ring box rolled towards the stove. As Melanie bent over to pick it up, Bart saw the flames behind her.

"Fire!" he pointed his finger and shouted.

She jerked up from the floor with the ring box in her hand. "Oh no, you don't!" she shouted. She shook the ring box at him. "This is mine! At last! You can yell about fires and floods and anything else you want to, but I've earned this! And come hell or high water, you can't take it away from me!"

She glanced at the stove and laughed insanely as she ran for the back door.

"YOU put the damn fire out!"

Bart staggered to the stove his panic attack forgotten. He prided himself on always being calm in other people's emergencies. Smoke filled the kitchen. He gingerly picked up the edge of the burnt dish towel he'd tossed away when he turned her around and kissed her. He dropped the towel into the sink and ran water over it. Then he leaned over the sink and started laughing. He laughed until he bellowed with it.

Melanie stood outside with her hand across her mouth, crying and laughing while his laughter filled the kitchen and rushed out the back door. They would be okay now; she knew it in her heart. It was the most she'd ever heard him laugh in his serious, earnest, sincere life. Their life would be good. She'd waited in the kitchen through three chocolate cakes and the fourth one was ready to frost before he finally made his move.

She'd seen the look of desperation on his face when he arrived for Christmas, and surmised that he was at last planning to pop the question. Her job was to furnish a place and time to for him to do it. She acted like she didn't suspect anything. She saw the hell he was going through. No pity allowed. It was ring time, so she went to baking. No Mercy.

After a while, Bart sighed in relief and puzzlement. Something was different. His chronic nervousness was gone. Somehow, he felt like it might be gone permanently. He glanced at the open back door. Where was Melanie now? It seemed like she was developing a bad habit of disappearing lately. He would have to have a gentle talk with her about it, and also about baking too many chocolate cakes. Why, there were three of them already lined up on the counter and a fourth partially frosted!

Curtains on windows must be made of matching, viable materials or the windows should be left bare.

Chapter 33. Luck and Courage

Lucian watched the snow drifting into the treetops from an attic window. The wild gardens and yard beneath the trees were deep with snow. The wrought iron railing further out at the cliff's edge stood tall and white with snow. The attic held things he was collecting. He felt complete with all that he was accomplishing. He glanced at his watch and grinned to himself. It was almost time to leave for Melanie's engagement party...

*

The small, gaily wrapped package arrived three days before Christmas. Melanie stared at the return address, then quickly ripped away the wrapping. She opened the small white jeweler's box and lifted out the thin, silver chain, and examined the half of a heart strung on it.

"Bart! Look! Our circle is becoming complete!"

*

Lucian picked up the mail on the hall table. He sifted through it until he came to the little, gaily wrapped package. He turned it over and looked at the return address. His hands shook as he tossed the rest of the mail back on the table. In his hurry, he never noticed the long, legal looking letter that slid to the back of the table and fell down behind it. The writing on the thick letter was in dark blue ink, and it bore a South Pacific return address.

He pulled on his coat and strode out into the falling snow. He didn't stop until he reached the iron fence above the cliffs. The roar of the surf below filled his ears as he tore off the wrapping and opened the small white box.

He lifted out the thin, silver chain with half an ancient silver heart on it and instantly knew she was the keeper of the missing half.

His little messenger! At last! He thought of the silly orange hair that was soft as a dove, the leotards and tunics with the animals running across them, her naïve beauty and eccentric, brave heart. He thought of her small, shapely hand resting in his, much like the two parts of the silver heart joined together.

He held the half of a heart, shielding it with his hand from the snow, turning it over and over. There were many flaws in it. This used heart was worn. It held experiences other people would never know about. It held a past in it, like the two of them. It was a valuable antique, old and priceless, like the two of them were to each other. It held ancient magic and future hopes, just as their souls did.

He lifted up the silver heart for the snow to bless, an ancient ritual asking for the coming of Goodness into the silver. Yes, he was a match for her. He was the other half of her heart. It would be him and her and whatever karma was in store for them from now on. The snow fell softly in sweet, peaceful flakes filled with never ending love around him as he lowered the silver heart and pressed it to his chest.

A thousand rhymes for a thousand different times lie within each square of cloth attached to a Traveler's wedding dress.

Chapter 34. Traveler's Weddings

The ancient music flowed from the Travelers' instruments, winding its way through the woods and across fields of wild red poppies and purple alliums. The fragrance of wood smoke and happy voices came from inside a circle of Travelers' wagons.

A tall, dark man with silver wings in his hair strolled across the sunny meadow, walking the same path his ancestor, Lucas Blizzard Solestone once walked. He glanced up at the blue sky. Today was the summer solstice. They'd stayed in Europe for the past few months, preparing for this day. They planned to stay here with family and watch the first snow of the season from this meadow.

Fate had drawn him back to his ancestral home, introduced him to his ancestors, and given him another chance. He was grateful. His heart became entwined with the many loves he discovered, old and new. His people's understanding, dark gentleness and humor mixed with common sense, made life simple for him, a thing he'd always needed. His heart was healed; his old hurts gone. He was ready for this new beginning.

The Travelers were gathered for the wedding. He looked at the circled wagons where they waited. He walked into the Travelers circle and took his place beside the other groom.

Both tall, rangy grooms wore traditional and elegantly cut black trousers made of the best materials the women in their families could procure. They wore hand sewn, long sleeved black shirts heavily pleated across the shoulders and cuffs. Red sashes were wrapped snugly around their waists.

The children of the brides watched the brides stroll through the meadow using the same path leading through wild red poppies and purple alliums to join their grooms. Both brides wore the traditional black wedding dress with many beautiful squares of cloth dancing on them.

Each square held a Traveler's history. Some stories were as old as the cross, some new, just as the people in their lives now were both old and new. The floating pieces of cloth whispered their stories and sang distant, wild, melodies as the brides strolled to meet their grooms.

One of the brides was tall and graceful. She wore her thick silver hair in a queenly coronet crowned with a circle of daisies and purple iris.

On her left hand rested a large, dignified moonstone ring.

The other bride was petite and curvy with short orange hair haloing her face. She looked like she owned stock in a tattoo parlor, for her skin danced with glowing lines. On her small, shapely hand was a black ring set in silver and flashing blue fire from its depths.

As Lucian Bellsted Solestone finished speaking the ancestral ritual words to her, "....and wherever thee travels, will thou forever think of us and keep our breadth and twain in thy own making?" he waited for her answer.

She completed the ritual words. "...and thee shall give just cause forever to us and ours."

In the dancing and feasting after the wedding, the grooms drew their brides into the center of the ring for the traditional wedding dance. They danced around the fire, pulled the red sashes from their waists, then wrapped them around their brides and themselves to let everyone know their wives were under the protection of the men in their family as well as their own.

Avalon's face glowed with delight and from the animal lines running over it. Her children whispered to each other, "Don't you think mother has enough tattoos? Maybe she should stop getting them. They look almost like they are moving....and now she says she might write a book on spiritual animal lore...and dedicate it to Harry somebody? That's just crazy!.... I do like the buffalo tattoo, though..."

"Well, you know how mother is. We'll just keep on overlooking her. I mean, she's so old and she seems to be happy. Who the hell gets married at her age except some kind of nut? Well, I guess happiness is what counts when you're that old."

Late that night, Lucian and Avalon slept under the blanket of stars spread out in the heavens above them. Dancing through the night around them was a glowing circle of spinning, whirling animal lines reaching up to the moon.

*

Under the same stars in a far-away land, a tall young woman with doe eyes and long, wavy hair stood on a moonlit beach, staring up at the moon with eyes as cold as black diamonds. She was thinking about the letter she secretly mailed to him half a year ago. He never answered.

"Lucy!" she heard Minnie calling.

"Coming!" Minnie shouted, turning away from the sea's everlasting noise. She was tired of it. Things were going to change. She would make them change.

"No, this isn't the end!" she whispered fiercely to herself, "it's just the beginning!" Silver lines arched up and curled across her face.

Patsy Stanley is an artist, illustrator and author. She has authored both nonfiction and fiction books including novels, children's books, energy books, art books and more.
If you enjoyed this book, check out the Desert Oasis Series!

Book One

Cowboy Johnson's Desert Oasis

Mama and the 57' Mercury

Fleeing a desperate situation in her 57' Mercury, Mama and her 12 year old daughter Geena head south to make a new life. In the middle of a desert in nowhere, New Mexico, they stop at a gas station and grocery store, formerly a little white church.

Parked in a 59' pink Cadillac convertible at the side of the store under the only shade tree for miles sits a woman crying loud enough to break the sound barrier. The store owner, the mysterious Cowboy Johnson, steps out and urges them to help her. Mama and Geena, both being psychics who specialize in appreciating land yachts, are hooked.

The adventures begin in book one with the gradual gathering of a group of lost, hiding out, secret laden, mostly psychic misfits living at the store.

When the store is full and running over with misfits, isolates and hermits, in self defense, William and Cowboy Johnson build a motel, restaurant, and gift shop and jokingly name it Cowboy Johnson's Desert Oasis.

309

The misfits build a life together, then move on, one after the other as time passes. But they return to the store each year for Christmas, back to the roots they grew together to celebrate and strengthen each other for the new year ahead.

An old fashioned read, one to be savored like a piece of hot chocolate cake, a story from an era of time rich in two lane blacktopped roads, land yachts, and the many endless roads leading to love.

Book Two
The Red Cactus Desert
Geena and the 59' Dodge Lancer

Book Three
The Three Cactus Limbo
Bud's Garage and the Quest of the Three Magi

Book Four
Away in a Desert
Susan Sugar Diamond

Book Five
The Desert Store
The Red Cactus orphanage

Book Six
Manfred's Folly
Timmon's legacy

www.ingramcontent.com/pod-product-compliance
Lightning Source LLC
Chambersburg PA
CBHW031622100726
47898CB00006B/1903